The
Boarding
Pass

Betty Gossell
Karen Pickens

authorHOUSE®

AuthorHouse™
1663 Liberty Drive
Bloomington, IN 47403
www.authorhouse.com
Phone: 1 (800) 839-8640

This is a work of fiction. All of the characters, names, incidents, organizations, and dialogue in this novel are either the products of the author's imagination or are used fictitiously.

Published by AuthorHouse 10/31/2017

ISBN: 978-1-5462-1214-0 (sc)
ISBN: 978-1-5462-1213-3 (e)

Library of Congress Control Number: 2017916335

Print information available on the last page.

Any people depicted in stock imagery provided by Thinkstock are models, and such images are being used for illustrative purposes only. Certain stock imagery © Thinkstock.

This book is printed on acid-free paper.

Because of the dynamic nature of the Internet, any web addresses or links contained in this book may have changed since publication and may no longer be valid. The views expressed in this work are solely those of the author and do not necessarily reflect the views of the publisher, and the publisher hereby disclaims any responsibility for them.

Praise for

The Boarding Pass

"I absolutely loved this book. I felt like I was there. Passed it on to my daughter." Roberta C.

"An easy-to-read look into the lives of passengers on a plane. I want to know more." Rosemary F.

"I loved this book! I TOTALLY am not a reader, but I couldn't put it down!!! Every chapter left me wanting more!!!" Karen H.

"It is an intriguing book. Didn't put it down till I finished it." Susan H.

"The book is a Fine Restaurant decadent dessert with a beautiful coffee! I want to take it slow and absorb - not dash through it! What a great concept. It's like a book you wish to read a page, then pause...not wishing it over." Tara S.

"Since reading this wonderful book, I now find myself gazing each time at many passengers on my flights and wondering where they are going and what their story might be. LOVED it!" Marlene F.

"Hard to put down! Only downside is that I found myself hooked on each person's story, and it left me wanting to read more about each of them. Guess that leaves room for the follow-up book(s)." Christie K.

"I found it to be very interesting! It left me hoping for more!" Wanda G.

"An interesting look into the lives of 8 people as they all go about their day, linked only by a shared airplane seat. Despite the brevity of our glimpse into their lives, you become invested almost instantly, and quickly find yourself wondering what happened to them after they got off the plane." Jackie D.

"Great story line! It would make a great movie!!" Mark L.

"Really enjoyed the book. It was well written." Carolyn R.

"It was a good read – You guys have the talent! Awesome!" Mary Sue R.

"A brilliantly written book about everyday people, but with a twist." Linda H.

Dedication

To my family and friends, who were always supportive of my dreams and encouraged me to never settle for less than my best;

To my co-workers and fellow road warriors, who know all too well the trials and tribulations of the crazy life that we lead;

But most of all to my fabulous daughter Karen. You have been the light of my life and my inspiration since before you were born. I never could have done this without you! I love you more!

Betty Gossell

To the Gossell and Pickens clans, for loving me as I am, for giving me more happy memories than anyone has a right to wish for, and for never being more than a phone call away;

To my friends, past and present, who shaped me and fueled me and made me better. Thank you for being beautiful and talented and forgiving;

To my wonderful husband Chris. I don't have enough words, and for me, that's saying something! You're the closest thing to perfect, and my life is immeasurably better with you by my side;

To my gorgeous daughter Lilah Joy. You are a dream come true, so bright and funny and challenging. You make me a better person every day. I'm so grateful that you're mine;

And of course, to my mother. You gave me life and you gave me so much of yourself that we're practically the same person sometimes. I love you more than you will ever know. I couldn't ask for a better mom or friend.

Karen Pickens

Foreword

The world and how we perceive it has changed drastically, even in my relatively short lifespan. The planet has gotten smaller and simpler to traverse. Stereotypes have been discarded and new ones erected. Definitions of success, family, happiness - all have undergone massive renovations, but there are a few truths that hold.

We still glorify the "special" moments in life, those with measurable quantities of interest. And we shun and almost dread the "ordinary." It seems that we must be reminded that even in the most exemplary life, a snapshot may reveal that which is static and mundane.

So how would it be possible to find a true cross-section of life amongst ordinary people? That would probably depend upon your definition of ordinary. Maybe it's running to the grocery store to pick up food for your family for the week. Maybe it's standing in line at the bank to deposit a paycheck. Maybe ordinary is pushing a lawnmower or a swing. Maybe it's sitting in a classroom, a traffic jam, or an airplane seat.

Though our actions and even our words cannot always be revolutionary, even the most cynical among us cannot deny that chance encounters and other so-called ordinary events have the potential to change our little piece of the world. These unsuspecting snapshots may not start or end a war. They may not crumble an empire or spark a new dream. But that they exist is cause for research into to the human condition, those warring desires for stability and change. Only a little dissection will show that everyone has a story – a past, a future. Every person has a place of origin and a destination, as well as somewhere in between. And somewhere on this journey, for every blessed one of us, there are moments - more frequently than you would expect - when we are the direct opposite of ordinary.

—Karen Pickens

Contents

Prologue

Jean

What a lousy way to spend her 50th birthday. Instead of celebrating a successful job interview in Dallas, Jean found herself jammed into the window seat on an overly-crowed and delayed flight back to St. Louis, sweltering in the 105 degree Texas heat.

She hated sitting next to the window, often feeling trapped into the small space by strangers who may or may not let her get up to stretch her legs. Ironically, this was much the same way she felt trapped by her life after years of questionable career decisions. She looked into the seat back pocket in front of her for anything she could use as a fan, and noticed something sticking out of the in-flight magazine. The crumpled piece of paper was a boarding pass for a woman named Lisa Davis, who flew from Des Moines to Chicago earlier that morning. Also folded neatly in the bottom of the pocket was today's *Des Moines Register*, open to the sports section.

Glancing at the boarding pass, she began to wonder about Lisa's life. Who was she? Where was she going so early in the morning? Was Lisa's life any more fulfilling than her own? Did she have a family or anyone to care if she made the trip, or care if she came back home? Jean turned the small piece of paper over and over in her hands, almost willing it to tell Lisa's story.

BOARDING PASS

PASSENGER RECEIPT 1 OF 1

Davis, Lisa

Davis, Lisa

DSM - ORD

Chapter One

Global Air

SEAT NUMBER

19F

Date and Time
JUNE 09, 2017
06:00 AM

Destination: ORD

Chapter One

DSM to ORD (Lisa)

The only light in the room was the soft red glow from the alarm clock. 1:57 AM. With a resolute sigh, Lisa slipped quietly from the warm bed she had shared with her husband Kevin for the past 27 years and walked silently across the room. The alarm was set to ring in a few minutes, but she turned it off so Kevin could sleep undisturbed. After a quick hot shower, she dressed in the clothes she had laid out the night before. Pulling her long blond hair into a pony tail, she applied a little bit of makeup and picked up her small red suitcase and matching carry- on bag. She paused at her bedroom door to blow a silent kiss in Kevin's direction. He was so handsome while he slept, and had to resist brushing her fingers through his tussled dark hair. She loved him so much, and leaving without saying goodbye was so difficult.

She walked quietly down the hall and glanced into the dark bedroom of their teenage son Shane. His long gangly frame was sprawled across his bed, and he was buried under a mound of covers. She tiptoed past Shane's door, trying to avoid tripping over the dog sleeping in the hallway. The Irish Setter was 15 years old now, and almost completely deaf. They had gotten him when Shane was little, and the two were inseparable. After making her way downstairs, she took one quick look around her recently remodeled kitchen to assure herself that all was in order. Shane had done a great job putting things away after his party last night. She looked in the fridge one last time and saw that it was well stocked with Kevin's favorites and Shane's necessities. Taking her cardigan from the hall closet, she turned off the lights and walked out the back door into the cool Iowa night. She had about an hour's drive to Des Moines before her 6 AM flight to Chicago. Even though it was early June, the air had a chill that made her wish for a warmer sweater.

The gravel in the driveway crunched under her tires as she backed her old Honda out of the garage. She paused to admire the large house that she and Kevin had worked so hard to restore after they first got married. As young teachers in the local school system, money was always tight. But they had found a run-down farmhouse on the edge of Winterset and worked nights and weekends for over a year to make it their own. Their first child, Miranda, was born just weeks after they moved in. Their son Tyler came three years later, and then Shane made his appearance just as Tyler was going to Kindergarten. Even in the dark she could see the outline of the basketball hoop on the driveway and the old swing set in the back yard. Her garden was growing well, and they had enjoyed their first vegetable pickings just last week. She inhaled the fresh country air, and knew this was the life she had always wanted. At the end of the driveway, she stopped and checked the box for the *Des Moines Register* and found that the delivery person had already been there. Tucking the paper in her carry-on bag, she turned from the driveway out onto the highway. She loved driving in the early morning, and left her window down just a bit to inhale the cool air, noticing the familiar and intoxicating scent of freshly mowed grass.

When she met Kevin all those years ago, they were both education students at the University of Iowa in Iowa City. Introduced by mutual friends, Lisa had fallen for Kevin's dark good looks and hazel eyes almost immediately. He was a star on the track team, and Lisa had been his biggest supporter in the stands. He graduated while Lisa was just a sophomore, and moved to Winterset to teach Jr. High math and coach the track team. Lisa was miserable being a few hours away from him, and they were married the weekend after her own college graduation two years later. Wearing her mother's ivory wedding gown, she proudly stood with Kevin to say their vows in front of a very small group of family and friends.

"I, Lisa, take you, Kevin, as my lawfully wedded husband, to have and to hold from this day forward." Lisa had said those words bravely but with a slight quiver in her voice. Looking into Kevin's eyes with love and trust, she had pledged her life and soul to him that day. Her sisters were beside her in their pale yellow bridesmaid dresses, and she held a bouquet of roses and daisies. Her mother wiped a silent tear from her eye, and her father gave her a wink of encouragement. But all she could really see was the amazing man she loved more than life itself.

"I, Kevin, take you Lisa." She heard his voice break and knew he was nervous about saying the vows just right. But no matter the words, she believed they were knit together with a bond that would last forever. As much as she had loved him then, it paled in comparison to her feelings for him today, so many years later. She glanced down at the ring he had put on her finger that day and knew that being Mrs. Kevin Davis was who she was meant to be.

She was fortunate to get a job teaching 4th grade at one of Winterset's two elementary schools, and she moved into Kevin's tiny apartment on the edge of town. They saved every spare penny for a full year before finding their "dream home" on a small piece of land just west of town. Their parents helped with the down payment and Kevin's dad (who owned a construction company) spent many weekends assisting with the major renovations. When they discovered that Lisa was pregnant with Miranda, Lisa was thrilled to spend her weekends fixing up the tiny nursery, decorating with Winnie the Pooh and Tigger. Kevin was nervous at the thought of being a father, but soon it was obvious that he was a great dad. He loved his children, and had built the swing set and a playhouse that they had all used for years. Now Miranda was a court reporter in Des Moines, and Tyler had just finished his junior year at Drake University; following in his dad's footsteps and staring on the track and baseball teams. Lisa was a bit disappointed that he did not move home this summer, opting instead to stay in Des Moines and work in the university's athletic department as an intern. But she understood his need to "spread his wings" a bit, and knew she would see him often in the coming year.

Shane, on the other hand, loved living at home. He was 17 now, and appeared to be in no hurry to leave. Like his dad and brother, he excelled in sports, especially baseball and wrestling. He hit a homerun in last night's game and drove in the winning runs. Lisa was glad she was able to see the game – this trip to Chicago had been planned for quite some time, but his game had been rescheduled because of rain the previous week. She stood in the stands and cheered as he rounded the bases and then listened to him retell the story later after he had gotten home. Several of his team-mates had come to the house after the game and were up late talking and laughing in the back yard. Lisa had gone to bed early, since she had this early morning flight, but Kevin had stayed up to supervise things. Shane had just started looking at colleges, but his heart had never really been on his studies. He loved fixing cars, and spent most of his free time rebuilding an old Chevy in his friend Tommy's garage.

The drive to Des Moines went quickly, and Lisa pulled into the almost deserted airport parking lot. After taking her bags from the car, she walked quickly into the terminal. There were few people awake at this time of the morning, so she did not have to wait in line to check in. The ticket agent was friendly and efficient.

"Where to, this early morning?" the young woman asked.

"Chicago, on the 6 AM flight," Lisa answered.

"I need to see your ID. How many bags are you checking?"

Lisa pulled her driver's license from her wallet, and handed it across the counter. "Just one bag." The agent quickly printed her boarding pass and tagged her suitcase. She handed her license and boarding pass back to Lisa, and set the suitcase on the conveyor belt behind her.

"You are all set, Ms. Davis – everything is on time, and you will be boarding in about an hour. Go down this hall and to your right. There is an escalator that will take you upstairs to security."

"Thanks so much, have a good day," Lisa answered. Picking up her purse and small carry-on, she moved away from the counter and slowly down the hall. They had remodeled this part of the airport since the last time she had been there, and she admired the changes. After riding up the escalator, she took her place in the short security line. Off came her shoes and sweater, and she put them in the gray tub for scanning, along with her purse and carry-on bag. After walking through the x-ray machine, she picked up her belongings and headed toward her gate. This was the first time she had flown in almost a year – actually, the last time was when she rushed to Chicago last fall when her mother Nancy had been critically injured in an auto accident. She had lived just a few days after Lisa got to the hospital; the drunk driver who hit her had walked away without a scratch. That flight was one of fear and worry; this one was supposed to be one of fun and friendship. So why was she dreading it so?

She sat alone in the boarding area and pulled a granola bar from her bag. Several colorful "Visit Chicago" flyers were tucked in the pocket of the bag, but she could not bring herself to open them. She hated being forced into uncomfortable situations, and feared that the next few days with her sisters would be extremely unpleasant. How she wished she could have found an excuse not to go today.

This trip had been the brainchild of her younger sister Susan. As the baby of the family, and the favorite of their parents, Susan seemed to do everything right. She married her childhood sweetheart 19 years ago, and was a stay-at-home mom for their twin preteen daughters. She lived in a cute little house just a few miles from where their parents had lived. She also had been the primary caregiver for their father during the final stages of his battle with Alzheimer's before he passed away just a month after their mother's accident. Lisa and Susan had always gotten along ok, but Lisa often felt alienated since she had moved so far away from everyone. Her busy school schedule, plus keeping track of a large house, garden, and three children, did not leave her much time for visits, and Susan commented more than once that she needed a break from the daily stress of caring for their aging parents. Lisa felt very guilty that she had not found a way to be more helpful during those stressful weeks, and months, and years.

Their older sister Rebecca was another story altogether. She and her husband Lawrence were partners in one of Chicago's largest and most prestigious law firms, and lived in an upscale condo on the waterfront. Too busy for children or pets, their hectic work and social schedules left little time for family or close friends. They chose not to have children, a concept foreign to Lisa who had trouble imaging a life without her children. They were the joys of her life, and she loved being a mom. Rebecca did handle the probate on both of their parents' wills, but had been too busy to spend much time with either of them in their final days. There was a certain level of friction between the sisters because of Rebecca's busy schedule and Lisa's inability to be of much help because of caring for her own family. Harsh words had been said at their father's funeral; words that left the sting of anger and frustration with all three sisters. Susan, in an effort to assume the role of peacemaker, had thought that the sisters should get together for some fun and to explore Chicago together. Hopefully this would be a start to mending their fractured relationships. Even though they had grown up in the Chicago area, they had never gone as sisters to do many of the "touristy" things that visitors from out of town usually did, and Susan was hoping the three girls could bond as sisters again.

"I think it will be so good for the three of us to spend some quality time together," Susan had said a few months ago, when they first started planning the trip. "We have not seen each other since the funerals, and I don't know about you, but I could use a little sister time about now."

Rebecca had been noncommittal, of course, saying she would have to see what her trial schedule was like, but would do her best to squeeze in some time for them. Lisa didn't have the heart to disappoint her little sister, and had reluctantly agreed. Susan was excited, and had planned four days of sightseeing and shopping. They even had tickets to an off-Broadway show for tomorrow night.

About 45 minutes before her flight, the gate agents arrived and took their place behind the small counter. Lisa double checked with them and found the flight was still on time. The gate area began to fill with other sleepy travelers, and before long, Lisa boarded the plane and settled into seat 19F. She enjoyed sitting by the window, and was hoping to catch a quick nap before landing in Chicago in a little over an hour. She knew that Susan would be at the airport to pick her up, but Rebecca had not returned her latest phone calls, so Lisa was not sure when they would meet up with her, if at all.

The flight attendants seemed overly perky for such an early hour of the day. Lisa admired the fact that they looked so 'pulled together' and glanced down at her own slightly frumpy travel outfit. She was just a few weeks short of her 50th birthday and was starting to look her age. Perhaps she should have spent a little more time on her own appearance today. Her khaki pants were rather rumpled, and her tan and green plaid tunic was comfortable but did little to camouflage her sagging curves. Her loafers were scuffed and well worn, and she could not remember how old they were. She tried to smooth the wrinkles from her slacks, but was sure that Rebecca would not have been caught dead in an outfit like this. For some reason, Lisa was always comparing herself to Rebecca, and usually felt that she came up short.

The plane was filling up now, mostly businessmen heading into Chicago for meetings, but also a few families dragging sleepy children along. A professional-looking Asian woman in an expensive and well-tailored business suit sat down in the aisle seat and slid her briefcase under the seat in front of her. Barely acknowledging Lisa's presence, she pulled a *Wall Street Journal* from her bag while talking on her Blackberry. Obviously there was important business to conduct, even at 5:30 in the morning. Lisa was relieved to be on summer vacation from school, and was looking forward to leisurely months with her husband and kids, and working in her garden. "Lisa's Secret Garden" as her kids loved to call it, had become a real joy to her, much to everyone's surprise. After growing up in the city with nothing but a few house plants, Kevin had been skeptical about her ambitions to grow her own vegetables. But after a few years of practice and some trial and error, her garden was now quite prolific. With Miranda and Tyler both living just an hour away in Des Moines, she knew she would see them often over the summer months. She and Kevin were even hoping to take a mini-vacation of their own without the kids this year; the first time since their 20th anniversary. They were not planning anything too fancy or expensive, maybe just a long weekend in Kansas City or Memphis. She was sure that Shane could spend the weekend with Tommy and she and Kevin would not have to worry about him. Kevin had the summer off from school, too, but had taken a part-time job at the local Home Depot to make a little extra money. They still had another year of tuition to help Tyler with, and Shane's senior year was coming up. There were always so many expenses involved with that.

Lisa sat up with a jolt when the reality of Shane's graduation next year sank in. One year from now, she would have no children at home, and she and Kevin would be starting a new phase of their life together. After all these years, they would be alone again. The big farmhouse was already starting to feel a bit empty, but Shane was a lively and funny kid who had helped to fill the voids left by Miranda and Tyler. The house certainly would be quiet after he left, IF he left, that is. He just might decide to stay around a little longer, and Lisa admitted that she would not mind. She really did enjoy being a mom.

The plane was in the air now, and the flight attendants passed out coffee and juice. Not even a muffin – things sure had changed in the past few years. Lisa remembered when you actually got a meal on a plane, but not anymore. She was glad she had that granola bar earlier. Once the announcement was made that it was safe to use electronic devices, the businesswoman near her started typing enthusiastically on her laptop. She sure was focused on her job! Lisa was glad to be on summer break and could let her brain rest for a while.

She pulled the *Register* from her bag and turned to the sports section. There was a nice write-up about Shane's homerun from last night, and Lisa could not help but feel pride for her younger son. There was even a picture of him rounding third base, one arm raised above his head and a fist pumping toward the sky. Lisa smiled as her fingers traced his outline in the paper. Oh, how she loved her children, all of them. Rebecca had no idea how much she was missing.

Lisa turned to the special section about the upcoming State Fair. She had been involved in 4H for most of her adult life, ever since moving to Iowa. This year she had been selected to serve as a judge for the bakery entries. Her specialty was in the pastry area, and she was excited to be named as one of the lead judges. Her kids used to tease her about being able to just "whip up a pie" when many of the other mothers at school could not even make a tolerable pie crust. It was just something that came easy to her, and she loved to experiment with different fillings and techniques. The crust recipe was a secret from her mother, however, and she refused to share it with anyone outside the family.

After finishing the paper, she folded it neatly and slipped most of it into the seat pocket in front of her, putting the Fair section into her bag for future reference. She could no longer ignore the fact that she was about to spend four potentially friction-filled days with her sisters. The unresolved tension between them had become even more obvious as time went on. Why Susan thought that forcing the three of them to spend "quality time" with each other would solve anything was beyond her. They were three very different people who had chosen three very different paths for their lives. Why could they not just leave things alone? She stared out the window and tried to quell the sense of dread she felt.

Lisa noticed the in-flight magazine in the seat pocket, and decided to read instead of thinking more about her dysfunctional family. She flipped through the pages without finding much of interest, stopping finally on the airport maps in the back. She never did like flying into Chicago O'Hare airport, and found the terminals a bit confusing. She was supposed to meet Susan at the baggage claim area, but Lisa was hoping to stop first at a coffee shop to grab something more substantial than her granola bar to eat. Her stomach had started to grumble, and she had no idea how long it would be before they had lunch. She loved fixing big breakfasts for her family, and wondered what Kevin and Shane would do without her today. She had left plenty of things in the fridge for while she was gone to Chicago, and Kevin had promised Shane at least one cookout on the grill with some of his school friends. There would be plenty of burgers and dogs, and probably a touch football game in the back yard. In fact, they were looking forward to a little time with just the guys, although there would probably be a few girls there, too. Shane was a really likable kid, and quite popular at school. She knew she had no reason to worry about them. But she missed them already.

The flight attendants collected the cups and napkins, and told everyone to put their laptops and IPods away. The businesswoman sitting on the aisle seemed annoyed that her work would have to wait a few more minutes. One again, Lisa felt a sense of pity for her, and was glad her life was not so stressed or high-pressured.

The pilot announced that they were making their descent into Chicago, and Lisa put the magazine away, not realizing that she had left her boarding pass tucked inside the back cover. Looking out the window, she scanned the familiar Chicago skyline and identified the Sears Tower and other landmarks. Once on the ground, she took her cell phone from her purse and called Kevin to let him know she had arrived safely. The businesswoman sitting next to her was back on her Blackberry again, checking for messages and emails. Kevin answered on the second ring, sounding sleepy and sexy. Even after all these years, she melted when she heard his voice, and couldn't wait to get home to see him again.

"Hi, honey. Did I wake you?"

"Mmmmm," he mumbled. "Where are you?"

"We just landed and I am waiting my turn to get off the plane. Go back to sleep – I just wanted to let you know that I got here OK."

"I'm glad everything was on time. Susan is picking you up, right?"

"Yes, she's gonna meet me at baggage claim. Have a good day honey. I'll call you later – I love you."

"Love you more…" he said sleepily.

Lisa put the phone back into her purse, made her way up the aisle and out onto the jet bridge. The "Blackberry Lady" was chatting away, rushing ahead of her. There were quite a number of people waiting in the gate area as she picked her way through the crowd and into the main terminal. After grabbing a biscuit at McDonald's and then stopping at the restroom to freshen up a bit, Lisa found the escalator that carried her down to the baggage claim area. It took her a few minutes to find the correct carousel, and then she saw Susan. They always did look so much alike, and bore a striking resemblance to their mother, who was fairly short but with lots of curves. Rebecca, on the other hand, looked much more like their father – tall and with striking, angular features. Too bad she did not have his caring and sensitive personality.

Susan was scanning the crowd, looking for Lisa, and then a big smile broke out onto both of their faces when they made eye contact. Lisa put aside her dread of the upcoming days to give her little sister a big hug. While waiting for Lisa's bag to arrive, Susan was bubbly and talked excitedly about the plans for the upcoming days. Lisa told Susan about Shane's game last night, and Susan filled her in about the twins' latest summer camp adventures. She then told Lisa that Rebecca was too busy to be there to meet her, but had promised to join them for lunch at a trendy restaurant in the Loop. She was in the middle of a big trial and was not sure how much time she would have for them over the next few days. Typical Rebecca.

Lisa's bag finally arrived, and after making their way through the crowd near the baggage claim area, the sisters walked toward the exit and out into the early morning Chicago sunshine.

Back at the gate area, Gerald MacNamara was boarding a flight to New York and wondering how he was going to survive the day.

STAPLE HERE

INSERT TEXT HERE

MacNamara, G

ORD - LGA

Chapter Two

Global Air

PASSENGER RECEIPT 1 OF 1

MacNamara, Gerald III

SEAT NUMBER
19F

Date and Time
JUNE 09, 2017
08:00 AM

Destination: LGA

Chapter Two

ORD to LGA (Gerald MacNamara III)

Oh, how the mighty have fallen. He might as well have that imprinted on his business card. For Gerald MacNamara III (Mac to his friends), those six words summed up his entire life—professional, personal, financial, and spiritual.

It was 6:00 AM and Mac was sitting dejectedly in the crowded boarding area at Chicago O'Hare airport, waiting to board his flight to New York City. This was his last chance, his only hope of saving his floundering architectural firm, which he'd not so modestly named Mac III. The recent housing bust had crushed his business and depleted his savings. But the final blow came a few months ago, when a messy audit turned up the unwelcome news that his CFO had been embezzling funds for the past three years. It was a crime that cut particularly deep considering he and Mac had been best friends since college.

Over five million dollars had been lost, and Mac's friend was facing up to forty years in jail. Although Mac had avoided any prosecution himself, he still faced the possibility of laying off workers and even closing his business for good. He had this one last chance to save his firm and his reputation. Quite literally, everything was resting on the presentation he was to make this afternoon to a group of investors who were interested in constructing a spectacular office building near the former World Trade Center site. Mac had the floor plans and elevation drawings in a crush-proof plastic tube, and his briefcase was filled with financial projections and testimonials from previous clients. He refused to take his hands off either of these, knowing how important they were. It was too bad that the sun hadn't even risen—Mac really needed a drink to steady his nerves.

He glanced subconsciously at his left hand and rubbed the place where his wedding ring used to be. His finger looked so different without the gold band that had been there for over twenty years, but the failing business and Mac's fondness for afternoon cocktails drove away the only person he had ever truly loved: his beautiful wife Misty.

Mac and Misty used to be the toast of the town, invited to all the exclusive parties and red carpet events. They thrived in a world of fast cars, expensive jewels, and the lavish lifestyle that came with being the CEO of one of Chicago's most prestigious businesses. Misty was ten years his junior and he had loved spoiling her with all the trappings of a trophy wife. They had just over two adventurous decades together, wild years of success and opulence, but when the market started to fail, Mac had to cut back on some of those luxuries, and Misty didn't take it well. She might have been more gracious about what she had to give up if he had given up his afternoon drinks in his home office. He never missed a Scotch and soda though, which later became mostly Scotch with very little soda, and then Scotch straight up. Mac became more and more withdrawn, and eventually Misty moved out of their bedroom into a spare room on the opposite side of their high-rise condo. And then she moved out altogether.

Within a week of her leaving, Mac was served divorce papers. His lawyer was appalled to find out that they'd never signed a prenuptial agreement, and that without working a day in her life, Misty would get half of everything. But even though she'd broken his heart, and even though half of everything wasn't all that much anymore, Mac would have gladly given her even more.

The architect and the socialite had met over twenty years ago at a Fourth of July party hosted by an up-and-coming real estate mogul. Mac was a rising star and Misty was the type of girl that always seemed to appear when rising stars congregated. She was a stunner, tall and blonde and curvaceous. He was average looking at best, but Misty seemed to genuinely like Mac. He fell hard for her, and would go on to tell anyone who asked that he was now a believer in love at first sight. He refused to consider that his money was the only thing keeping someone so young and beautiful at his side, but that didn't stop him from lavishing all he could upon her. Within months of their first meeting, he proposed with a massive diamond ring. They were married in a candlelight service on Christmas Eve in front of hundreds of guests. Their honeymoon was a cruise in the Mediterranean and a week in the south of France.

Mac's business really began to take off, and Misty was excited to play the gracious hostess. He could count on her to throw posh parties and invite all the A-list celebrities she could find. Every few years they moved to a larger and more luxurious home, filling it with clothes and trinkets purchased on their many international vacations. But the busier Mac got at work, the more he worried that Misty would be lonely at home. Due to a surgery she'd had after a boating accident when she was a teenager, Misty was unable to have children. Mac suggested that they adopt a child, but Misty swore that she was fine on her own and refused even the company of a dog or cat. She claimed that she didn't feel cut out to be a mom and Mac had grieved this decision in his own way, but now, he supposed it was the right call. He couldn't imagine navigating this tumultuous phase of his life with a child or two in the mix.

He supposed it was possible that being a father might have held him together when the stock market crashed and he was trading lavish vacations for long hours trying to salvage his company. But more than likely, any child of his would have been just as neglected and frustrated as Misty was when their lifestyle suffered. And just like Misty, this fantasy child would fail to see the severity of their situation, and would hold him accountable for things far out of his control.

Without children, Mac had made his business his true legacy, and had nurtured it over the years. To see it hanging on by a thread now was agonizing. If the men and women he met with today didn't see potential in his designs, if they didn't hire him, it was all over. His mouth went dry at the thought.

Mac glanced at his watch. He'd been concerned about delays when he learned that he wouldn't be on the first flight of the morning, but was pleased to see his plane arriving right on time from wherever it had been in the pre-dawn hours. He pulled his boarding pass from his suit pocket and his mood sunk even further. Seat 19F. Coach. Back of the plane. His ticket felt like a badge of dishonor for a man used to flying in private jets, or First Class if he was forced to fly commercial. Now he was just like the average people around him, only from the occasional bursts of laughter and the hum of excited chatter, they did not have the feeling of impending doom that he had.

After a crowd of sleepy passengers piled off the plane and the flight attendants took a moment to tidy up and restock refreshments, the gate agent announced that they were ready for First Class boarding. Mac instinctively stood and then self-consciously dropped back into his uncomfortable chair. With gritted teeth, he waited his turn and filed along with the fidgeting babies, sleepy teenagers and over-caffeinated businessmen. Slowly they marched through the drafty jet bridge and into the metal fuselage of the plane.

As Mac shuffled past the First Class passengers, already comfortably seated and with drinks in hand, he looked down at the floor, trying not to make eye contact. The last thing he needed was for one of these elite flyers to recognize him. There had been enough rumors and gossip about him and Misty in the local tabloids. Wouldn't they just love to know he was now flying Coach?

Further and further toward the back of the plane he went. It felt like a different planet back here. He gently put his document tube in the overhead bin and slid his briefcase under the seat in front of him. Crawling into his window seat, he noticed the lack of leg room. At just shy of six feet, he wasn't overly tall, but still felt like his knees were up under his chin and wondered how he would survive this two hour flight to New York.

Mac leaned his head against the cool window and closed his eyes. Air travel didn't really frighten him, but anxiety about his meeting had heightened his discomfort. The whining of the engines and the stale taste of the recycled air had him wishing that all of his senses could be dulled for a few hours. Maybe then he could get the rest he needed on this flight. He might have actually dozed for a few moments when he felt someone moving beside him, heard the buckling of a seatbelt. Sitting up slightly, he glanced to his left and almost cried out. The young woman beside him reminded him forcefully of Misty as she had looked so many years ago. She had long, slim legs and a tumble of golden hair and a movie star smile when she made eye contact with him.

"Sorry, I didn't mean to wake you," she said in a hushed voice.

"You didn't, don't worry," he managed to say. He knew it would be impolite to keep staring at her, but she just kept smiling. The more he looked, the less she really looked like Misty except for the hair. This girl's eyes were a greenish-hazel, not blue, and she was wearing a t-shirt and distressed jeans and sturdy boots, which Misty never would have done.

"Was that your big plastic tube thing in the overhead compartment?" she asked boldly, kind of out of nowhere.

Mac gave a little laugh. "Yes, it's mine. Was it in the way or something?"

"Oh, not at all," the young woman assured him. "I was just wondering what was in there. Are they super-secret government documents or maybe blueprints for a building you're going to rob?"

Mac couldn't help but chuckle loudly. "I think you've read a few too many novels. It's nothing as glamorous as that. I'm an architect and those are my design plans."

He expected her to be underwhelmed, but she seemed plenty impressed. "That's very cool. I thought about being an architect when I was younger. But someone told me they are the most boring students on a college campus because all they do is draw non-stop."

Mac grinned. "Your friend is right about that. No time for beer parties or extracurricular things in design school. It's worth it though, when you see your first building on the skyline."

The girl's pretty hazel eyes got a bit sparkly at his words. "I'd love that, to leave a legacy somehow. I've been accepted to UIC in the fall, which I suppose is a good start."

Mac's eyebrows rose a bit. The University of Illinois at Chicago was no joke. "Congratulations. What do you plan to study?"

"Bioengineering," she replied in a matter-of-fact tone. Then she smiled warmly at Mac's perplexed expression. "It's what you pick to major in when you can't decide between biology, chemistry, or computer science."

Mac let out a grunt. "You've just named every subject I would choose to never take again in school."

She giggled. "You sound like my dad."

Mac winced. He'd forgotten for a moment how much older than this girl he was. She was probably just eighteen. He could easily be her father; in fact, if he and Misty had been able to have a biological daughter, she would probably look just like this young woman. "Well, I'm sure your father is very proud of you."

"He is," she said softly, looking past him then out the window. Without Mac really being aware of it, the plane had taxied away from the terminal and was now racing down the runway. A moment later, after a second of weightlessness followed by a little swoop as gravity kicked back in, they were airborne, climbing up into the early morning sky.

To his surprise, the girl began to giggle quietly, trying to stifle it with her hands over her mouth. "What's so funny?" Mac asked.

"I just can't believe I'm actually doing this!" she gushed. "I've never left the country before!"

Mac frowned. "You know this plane is only going to New York, right?"

She rolled her eyes at him. "Yes, but I'm catching a connecting flight. I'm going to Spain! I can't believe it!"

Catching on, Mac nodded at her. "I love Spain. My wife and I went many times."

"Oh, that's lucky! How long have you been married?"

"Um, we were married for about twenty-three years. And we've been divorced for about eighteen months now, I guess."

The girl's eyes went wide and she looked so devastated at his words, like she'd never heard of something so sad in her life. "That's awful. We don't have to talk about her if you don't want to. We don't have to talk at all, I guess. I'm just feeling excited and chatty. I'll just read or something."

"You're not bothering me," Mac said gently. "Misty and I were great together, but she had expensive tastes and I've had a run of bad luck lately. Hopefully I can turn that around today."

"And then you'll try and win her back?" the girl pressed, staring openly at him.

Mac felt his brow furrow and he turned away from her. "I can't say that I've thought about that. I don't think she'd take me back."

"Well, I don't think it's very fair of her to only love you if you're rich, but if you became rich again, doesn't that mean that she would love you again?"

Mac grinned sadly. "What's your name?"

"I'm Tess," she said sweetly and reached over the armrest to shake his hand.

"Hi Tess, I'm Mac. And it's sweet of you to think that getting back with my wife would be that easy, but it's a lot more complicated than me making some money."

"Oh, I'm sure," Tess said. "When I was little, my parents had money troubles and it really brings out the worst in people. When you're tired from working or looking for work, and you're hungry and stressed, it just takes all of your flaws and puts them under a magnifying glass."

It was easy to brush away Tess's words, to minimize them because of her age and inexperience, but honestly, Mac found her story to be very accurate. Mac had always been a drinker, and under the microscope of financial instability, that particular vice had become his most prominent character trait. His kindness and generosity, his creativity and his drive, all of that had fallen aside in favor of his addiction.

So no, it had never been difficult to see why Misty left, how he had driven her away. But it shocked him how until this very moment, he'd never considered trying to win her back. When the divorce papers had showed up at his office, he'd seen that as the end of the line. He'd given her everything she'd asked for and hadn't put up a fight. Now he was wondering if that had been the right play.

"I'm really sorry if I overstepped," Tess said, knotting her fingers together and looking worried.

"No need to apologize, I was just thinking," Mac mumbled. "Why don't we change the subject? Tell me about what you're going to do in Spain."

Tess's lips turned up in a smile. "El Camino Santiago," she said, her accent very precise and her tone very dreamy.

"You're going to Spain to buy a car?"

She gave a musical little laugh at that and slapped his arm playfully. "No! It means The Way of St. James. I'm going on a seven-day spiritual hike in Northern Spain. It's a pilgrimage, a time of prayer and discipleship and reflection. I'm giving myself fully over to God before I fall into my studies at UIC. I don't want to lose sight of Him in that critical time, so I'm sort of stockpiling some time in His presence. I'm not sure if that makes any sense…"

Mac gave her a vague nod. He had never been a religious man, had always been too busy seeking after worldly pleasures to bother much with church or God. Tess made it sound very romantic, but beneath her thirst to explore a foreign country, Mac could detect a deep maturity. Her faith was youthful and fresh but not naïve. It wasn't as off-putting as he might have expected it to be.

"I'm not sure it totally makes sense to me," he admitted. "But it sounds very nice." He looked up then to see the flight attendant nearing with the beverage cart. All at once, his throat went very dry again. He'd been waiting for this. He'd fully intended to purchase an alcoholic drink when the time came, but now he wondered if Tess might not approve. She was not his wife or his daughter of course, but he'd begun to value her opinion of him. He knew all Christians weren't teetotalers, but he wasn't sure he ought to risk it. She had an optimism and a spirit about her that was refreshing after so many months of depression and foreboding, and he didn't want to disrupt that. And then of course, he had the meeting of his life this afternoon. He knew all too well how one drink to calm the nerves soon became six to drown out the sorrow and pain of the day. So he asked for a coffee instead.

Tess simply asked for water and spent the next several minutes sipping quietly and munching on her complimentary pretzels. Mac thumbed through the seatback pocket and pulled out what he expected to be the *USA Today,* but it seemed he would have to make do with the *Des Moines Register,* something left behind by an earlier passenger apparently. He found the financial section mildly entertaining for a while, and circled a few interesting stock prices, but found himself glancing over at Tess every now and then. Unlike most girls her age, she didn't seem to have a phone with her to play with, and while she wore an expression of calm, it seemed a bit forced. Several minutes later, when the trash from their little snack had been collected, Tess seemed ready to burst if she didn't speak, so Mac pocketed the newspaper and asked her to tell him more about her upcoming trip.

For most of the remainder of the flight, the two studied a paper map Tess had brought that showed the sixty miles she would be covering over the next week. Mac listened to her itinerary and asked questions about what would happen with her luggage and where she would sleep. It amused him that though the nature of the pilgrimage seemed to be a return to old-time methods for travel and one-on-one communion with God, each night was spent in a nice hotel or bed and breakfast along the route, and most of her meals were to be prepared by high end Spanish chefs.

It wasn't until the plane was beginning its initial descent that Tess brought up Misty again. She wasn't pushy about it, just simply asked about their first meeting. Mac was happy to relay that story, when he'd first seen her on the steps of a beautiful Chicago manor house. The setting sun had turned her golden hair a molten coppery color and he'd fallen in love with her right there.

"That sort of love can fade out," Tess said wisely. "It burns bright and fast and if you don't fan those flames, they can die. But I can tell that you still care for her. I don't know what pushed her away, but you owe it to yourself to fight for her."

Mac grinned patiently. "And what do you know about bright, burning love?"

She gave him a sweet smile. "The Bible teaches about all the different kinds of love. I'll be ready when the right boy comes along."

"I'm sure your dad can't wait for that!"

Tess laughed for quite a while at that one. When the plane landed and she was retrieving her bag, she brought his document tube down for him and handed it over. "Are you sure there aren't any secret plans in there?"

"I'm afraid not," Mac said. "Maybe one day you'll see a chic little office building in New York designed by the rich and famous Gerald MacNamara III, and it will be our little secret that you knew him back when he was poor."

"Oh, Mac. Poor is an attitude, and one that you don't have," Tess assured him. "I'll say I knew you back when you were broke and on the outs with your wife. How about that?"

"I think that sounds pretty great. Take care in Spain, Tess."

"I will. Good luck today!" And she melted into the crowd, leaving him to walk down to the cab stand alone. Mac took a deep breath, tasting the subtle difference in the way the New York air felt in his lungs. It wasn't the cleanest feeling in the world, but it was full of promise. As he waited his turn for a taxi, he thought that regardless of how his meeting went today, maybe it was time to give Misty a call. In fact, he thought perhaps a call was long overdue.

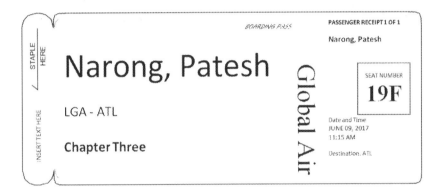

STAPLE HERE

INSERT TEXT HERE

BOARDING PASS

Narong, Patesh

LGA - ATL

Chapter Three

Global Air

PASSENGER RECEIPT 1 OF 1

Narong, Patesh

SEAT NUMBER

19F

Date and Time
JUNE 09, 2017
11:15 AM

Destination: ATL

Chapter Three

ORD to ATL (Dr. Narong)

Dr. Patesh Narong sat patiently in his window seat 19F, reading the latest *Journal of American Medical Association* about an emerging strain of the Ebola virus. He had co-authored the article, and was pleased with the clarity of the details and the effectiveness of the charts and graphs. The article was even featured on the cover of the magazine, which was a quite a coup. As a researcher, Dr. Narong had been very successful in developing and testing vaccines for some of the more challenging diseases of the 21st century.

In fact, it was that success that had led to today's flight. The CDC in Atlanta had learned of his latest research, and had read an advance copy of the article. They begged him to come to the CDC to head up their Ebola project, and offered prestige and notoriety that was hard to refuse. He had packed up his office in Manhattan, shipped his meager belongs to a storage facility recommended by his real estate agent, and boarded the plane to Atlanta where he was told he would be participating in a press conference soon after arriving at the airport. This sure was a long way from his humble beginnings in a poor village in India.

He was born the third of nine children (but the oldest son), and life was very hard for everyone in his family. Food and water were often scarce, and Patesh never believed that his dream of becoming a doctor could ever come true. But one day while he was attending the local missionary school, a special visitor from the US spoke about a medical school in Chicago that was offering full scholarships to students who were willing to train in the US and promise to remain in America for ten years, practicing in poor inner city areas or entering specialties such as research or pathology. Patesh talked to his parents about the idea later that night, and within a few months he had flown to Chicago to begin his studies. He spoke virtually no English at the time, and felt very isolated from most of the students. He studied hard and excelled in his classes, but was quite lonely and spent most of his time alone in the library. Graduation and residency followed, and then a research position at a top hospital in New York City. He had been able to take a few short trips back to India to see his family, and felt the culture shock of the extreme poverty of his village versus the excesses of the Big Apple. He did send as much money as he could to help things out at home, but never felt that it was enough. He felt guilty for this success and for their struggles.

When his ten years of obligation were over, his family had urged him to return home to help solve the various health crises brought on the crushing poverty. He struggled with the decision for quite a while, but then decided that his skills could be better utilized in a facility with top- notch funding and equipment. Of course, any vaccines or drugs that he developed would be of a benefit to everyone, including those in India.

His family did not understand his decision, and a silent rift grew between them.

"Son, you have a duty to come home. You are the oldest son and have a responsibility to your family. Your people need you. Your family needs you. How can you justify your lavish lifestyle when you spend more money each day for your coffee than we do on food the entire week?" His mother pleaded with him to return to India and work with the government to help solve the poverty crisis.

The years passed, and Patesh's reputation as an impeccable researcher continued to grow. He had taken English lessons in his spare time, and had become quite proficient with the language. He worked doubly hard to lose most of his accent that he felt would stereotype him and hold back his career. Of course, his family disapproved and felt he was becoming too westernized.

He was quite handsome, in the dark and brooding sort of way typical for those of his heritage, and at 5 feet 11 inches, he was a bit taller than his father. Although he was a naturally shy and reserved young man, his long hours in the lab prevented him from having much of a social life. One of his co-workers, a long-legged blond named Stephanie, had tried in vain to get him to notice her for more than her expertise with a microscope, but Patesh seemed blind to her charms. He lived in a tiny efficiency apartment within walking distance of his office, but spent very little time there. The walls were bare and the tiny loft contained few clues as to the personality of the person who lived there. He actually had very little to pack once the call from the CDC came.

The plane began to fill, but both seats beside him remained empty. How nice to have three seats to himself! He smoothed a few stray wrinkles from his slacks and adjusted his tie. He wanted to look impeccable for the cameras at the press conference.

Just as the doors of the plane were about to close, a young man in his middle to late 20's came rushing in and hurried down the aisle to stop at row 19. Tossing a small bag into the overhead bin, he sank into the aisle seat. Almost immediately, the plane pushed back from the gate. "Wow, just made it!" he exclaimed in a thick southern drawl to no one in particular. He turned to Patesh and said, "My flight from Maine was late and I was just sure I would miss my connection!"

Patesh smiled politely in his direction, and turned his attention back to the article. It was as if all of his life had been in preparation for this moment, this position of importance with the CDC. Not bad for a poor kid from the dregs and lowest caste (the Shudra) in India. He was mentally practicing his comments for the press conference, trying to quell his nerves a bit. Even though he knew all the facts of his research by heart, he reviewed them over and mover, making sure of every last finding and statistic. He was never one for the spotlight, and had made few public speeches. The anticipated sea of TV cameras was a bit intimidating to him.

"So, where are you going today?" the young man asked Patesh. "I've been in Maine on a business trip – I'm a marketing rep for a trucking company, and we have a BIG client in Portsmouth who was threatening to go with a different company, someone more local. It was all I could do to try to save this big account, but I'm glad to be going back to Atlanta. Two days is way too long for me to be away from my wife and kids. Twins – age 3. What a handful!"

Patesh knew there would be no peace and quiet on this plane today. Mr. Chatterbox here was going to see to that.

"Gina – that's my wife – she stays home with the kids all day and I usually try to help in the evenings so she can have a break and a little time for herself. She's been alone with the twins for over 48 hours now, and is climbing the walls! Here's a picture she sent me just this morning." He put his cell phone on airplane mode to show Patesh a picture his wife had emailed to him earlier. "It's a picture of the kids eating breakfast today, with cereal on their heads and milk all over the table! What a mess!"

Patesh quietly closed his magazine and slid it into the seat pocket in front of him, alongside a newspaper someone on a previous flight had left. Perhaps if he made a point of reading the newspaper this guy would be quiet and leave him alone?

Pulling the *Register* from the pocket, Patesh saw that it was open to the financial section, and many of the stocks were underlined or circled. Someone sure had been very interested in the stock market today. Patesh turned to the health section, and was distressed to see a report of a new epidemic predicted to sweep Southeast Asia in the coming months. This virus was a mutation of a strain that Patesh had worked on a few years ago, but had somehow become resistant to the standard antivirals being used. If he was still in the clinic in New York, perhaps he would be able to shift his focus to include this new virus, or seek funding for hiring additional researchers. But now his hands would be tied with the Ebola research for months and maybe years to come.

"What? Oh, I'm sorry," Patesh finally answered. "I am on my way to Atlanta to work for the CDC doing research on viruses.

"Wow, that sounds important! You must be quite a famous guy, right?"

"No, not really. Or maybe just in my small circle of researchers.

Not many people know what we do or really care. They just want vaccines to protect their kids and grandparents. They have no idea what all is involved before the vaccines or other medications hit the shelves."

"I suppose. My name is Andy, by the way. Have lived in Atlanta all my life. You can probably tell that by my accent. Do you have someplace to live?"

"The HR people from the CDC have arranged for a corporate apartment for me for a month or two until I find something permanent. Since most of my time will be spent in the lab, I just want something close where I can walk or take the bus."

"So, no wife and kids to come with you? Or are they already in Atlanta waiting for you?"

"No, no wife or kids. I have been much too busy for that kind of distraction."

"Tell me about it! Sure has been hard to climb the corporate ladder when your wife is expecting twins and then they are born three months early. Or when they both come down with the chickenpox at the same time. I even had to pass up a promotion because it would have meant moving to Phoenix and all of our family is in Georgia. Plus, we are really involved in our local church. So, where is the rest of your family......parents? Brothers and sisters?"

"My father passed away last year, but my mother and my siblings still live in a small town outside of Delhi, India, where I was raised."

"India? Wow, you sure are a long way from home. Sorry about your dad. You must get really lonely being so far from home……"

Patesh shifted his weight in his seat a bit, and looked down at the newspaper. This stranger, this ANDY person, was getting way too personal and digging into places that Patesh had not wanted to look for a very long time. Yes, he was lonely. Much more lonely than he wanted to admit to anyone, especially a stranger on an airplane. From the time he was in medical school and did not know enough English to make many friends, he had retreated to his books and lab experiments as a way to push that loneliness away. Even after learning English, he had remained a loner. But now this guy was ripping that wound open, and his constant chatter was like pouring salt into it. How was he going to get this guy to change the subject? Or stop talking altogether?

His reprieve came in the form of a frazzled flight attendant passing out drinks and offering granola bars for sale. Patesh's request for a cup of hot tea was met with a frown and a roll of her eyes that told him he should have asked for a coke instead. He finally got a cup of hot water and a tea bag, but was hesitant to ask for some sugar and a little milk. He unwrapped his snack and sipped the hot drink, letting his mind drift back to the streets of India and the ever-present crowds and squalor. How different his life would have been if he had never left. So why the nagging thoughts now, of all times? Why was he feeling so unsettled? He was on the verge of something more important than anyone had ever dreamed of. Should he leave it now to return home? Where could he do the most good for mankind? Was there really a way to balance his demanding career and find a little peace and happiness for himself?

Andy finished his snack and started chatting again about the best places to visit in Atlanta and his season tickets to the football team, but Patesh was not really listening. Each minute brought them closer to

Atlanta, closer to this amazing opportunity. Closer to this new chapter of his life.

Patesh let his mind wander back to his first airplane flight. He was 17 and on his way to Chicago to start his medical studies. Two young men from his village were in the seats beside him. None of them spoke much English or had been more than a few miles from home. They barely spoke or moved from their seats the entire long flight from India. When the plane touched down in Chicago, they stood in awe, staring at the people and the sights of the big city. The director of the medical program was at the gate to meet them, along with an interpreter. They were escorted to the dorms and introduced to a few other foreign students. Patesh truly was a stranger in a strange land. He had immersed himself into his studies, always feeling the burden of responsibility and duty to his family and his country.

The flight attendant asked them to put away their carry-on items and to prepare for landing. Patesh was still looking for some sort of sign, something that would help him make the right decision. He looked again at the cover of *JAMA* and saw his name in print. He knew his family would be so pleased to get the copy that he had mailed to them. As the plane approached the airport, he looked at Andy and said, "I'm sorry, what did you say?"

"I said I really admire you and your dedication to your work. Not everyone could give up so much to devote their lives to serving others like you do. But anytime you want a home-cooked meal or to watch a game or something, give me a call. Here's my card – I know my wife would love to meet you. And she would be the first to let you know that her older sister Gloria is a nurse at a local hospital and SINGLE. I really think you two would have a lot in common."

"Thanks, Andy, that means a lot to me. I don't have a new card with me, of course, and will be very busy for a while. But I appreciate the offer."

After a moment or two of silence, Patesh turned to Andy and asked, "Do you ever regret your decision to put your family ahead of your career?

Do you wonder what things might have been like if you had moved to Arizona?"

Andy did not hesitate with his answer. "No, I'm so glad I put my family first. The career will always be there, my wife and kids may not be. I would not miss the chance to watch my twins grow, and Gina is the love of my life. So, I'm not making as much money as I could have, but at the end of the day, I'm one lucky guy."

Patesh turned his gaze toward the window and watched the Atlanta skyline come into view. He strongly wished he felt better about the decision he was about to make.

The landing was rather bumpy and the plane came to an abrupt stop on a runway far from the terminal. The pilot came over the loud speaker to tell the passengers that there had been a mechanical problem with the plane at their gate, and that they would be delayed for a few minutes. Andy turned on his cell phone and called Gina to tell her he would be a little late getting home.

"Wow, you should have heard the commotion in the background," Andy said when he hung up the phone. "She sure sounded exhausted. The twins are just getting over the stomach flu and everyone is pretty irritable."

Patesh turned on his cell phone and saw that he had a text message from the CDC Director, telling him that the press was waiting for him to deplane. Even before he could respond, the plane began to move and they taxied toward their gate. When it was finally their turn to leave their seats, Andy retrieved his bag from the overhead bin and said, "Good luck to you doctor. I know you have an important job ahead of you, and millions of people are counting on you."

"Thanks, Andy. I just hope I am up to the task. It has been a pleasure talking with you."

With that, the doctor walked off the plane and into a waiting throng of TV cameras and reporters. Andy stood off to the side and watched in amazement as Patesh took his place at the podium and began to speak.

"Thank you all for being here today. My name is Dr. Patesh Narong, and I am pleased to stand before you today to make an announcement. My journey to Atlanta and the CDC began almost 30 years ago in a small village in rural India...."

BOARDING PASS

Sullivan, Joel

Sullivan, Joel

Global Air

SEAT NUMBER

19F

ATL - DFW

Date and Time
JUNE 09, 2017
02:07 PM

Chapter Four

Destination: DFW

Chapter Four

ATL to DFW (Joel)

Women just love a man in uniform. This fact had always rather embarrassed Joel, whether back in his jock days or now as a soldier. But he couldn't deny that it was helpful today.

The female cab driver had refused to let him pay for his quick jaunt from the Army base down to Columbus. The woman at the Greyhound station had "accidentally" forgotten to charge him for his last-minute ticket to Atlanta. And the lady at the airport check-in had obligingly put him on the 'first available' flight to Dallas, after he'd heard her tell the couple in front of him that nothing was heading anywhere in Texas until later that night.

He fidgeted with anxiety as the woman printed up his ticket. The change in his plans went against his very un-spontaneous nature, but it had been necessary. It had been impossible to sleep last night on the base for three reasons. First, he was ridiculously jet-lagged. The hours from Baghdad to Georgia were nearly reversed, making it uncomfortable to lie down at what would normally be his noon. Secondly, sleep brought dreams, and ever since the incident with Pete...his dreams had not been pleasant ones. And lastly, there was Kristen. The beautiful girl he'd left back home was only a few hours away from him now. Being back on the same continent had made him restless. To be back in America, lying on his back in bed, and not feeling her resting on his shoulder—it was just wrong. As sleep evaded him, he'd stared at a photo of her, trying to find comfort in her wide green eyes and her tumble of chestnut hair. But her smile made him impatient.

So he'd bailed early, refusing to wait until tomorrow night when she arrived. She'd be so surprised! Her face would light up even brighter than the woman's behind the counter, whose brown eyes had gone all sparkly since he'd smiled at her.

Yes, women were naturally drawn to him in his fatigues, following him surreptitiously with their eyes as he moved with innate confidence, which was only partly for show. He had a good face, clean cut and honest. He was a poster boy for the young American hero. Women would moan and groan about not needing a man to take care of them or rescue them, but they gravitated to heroes. It was some bizarre genetic response.

It seemed that the only female who hadn't responded favorably to Joel was the girl sitting next to him in seat 19E. But she was a freak. Well, okay, that's not totally fair, but she certainly *looked* like a freak. She and the nondescript businessman in 19D had shuffled aside to let him into the window seat, and he'd had a hard time not starting at her. After the utterly foreign quality of war, he found it amusing that a young girl, eighteen years old at best, could startle him. She was of average height, willowy, and had probably been pretty once before dyeing her hair a jet black so severe, it was nearly indigo. Her eyes were heavily outlined in black liner and shadow, standing out harshly against her luminous pale skin. Dressed all in black, with a spike of metal through her left eyebrow, she was terrifying. Joel was uneasy sitting next to her, and ignored her thoroughly as the plane taxied and took off.

He opened his book, trying to sink back into the words he'd been reading on the bus, but they wouldn't take. His eyes kept migrating to Kristen's picture, which served as the bookmark for the battered paperback. Her sweet face, so unlike the stranger's next to him, gave him peace and butterflies all at once.

He gave up on the book after a few minutes, rifling through the seat pocket and finding an Iowa newspaper, left by some previous passenger. It seemed totally random, but then again, everyone flies these days – even corn farmers. He amused himself for several miles with the small town baseball scores, finding it hard not to reminisce back to easier times when a clear blue sky meant excellent baseball weather and wasn't about visibility from enemy spy planes. To try and quell the unpleasant thoughts, he worked the puzzle in the back of the in-flight magazine. Someone else had started it, but he was pleased to add a few answers of his own. Each person on this plane seemed to be adding a bit to the puzzle, much like life, he guessed.

He nursed a soda when the refreshment cart came along, gasping at the revelation of having ice in his glass. How many months had he guzzled eighty-degree water and been grateful for it?

It was after he'd munched the last of the ice cubes that he be- came aware that the girl next to him was angled slightly toward him, staring at him. From the corner of his eye he watched her gaze move from his large hands to his fatigue pants tucked into standard issue boots. Up to his suntanned face and closely buzzed sandy hair. From the book he'd tucked between his right thigh and the wall of the plane then up to his face again.

He turned his head toward her slowly, eyebrows raised expectantly. This was the mute equivalent of saying "What are you staring at?"

He waited for her pale cheeks to flush, or for her to turn away in embarrassment, but she surprised and terrified him again by keeping her blue-violet eyes trained on him. Long seconds ticked on and she simply cocked her head to the side as though studying something of interest under glass.

Hating to break first, Joel gave a resigned sigh. "Was there something you needed?" he asked tightly.

She watched him for another long stretch of seconds before flicking her eyes to his left wrist. "What's with the rubber band?"

His right hand went automatically to his wrist, fingering the thick rubber band that he wore like a bracelet. The skin beneath was bright red. He smirked, wondering why he felt compelled to explain this bizarre little detail to a stranger. But she had noticed it, and commented on it before asking all the basic questions that normally come up when a civilian sits next to a soldier.

"It's to keep me from swearing," he said rather sheepishly. "Hanging around a couple dozen guys who use the worst language imaginable...it rubs off after a while. And my parents are real salt-of- the-earth type of people. When I came home from boot camp sounding like a sailor, they nearly tossed me out. So I'm training myself to quit cussing. Every time I swear, or feel like swearing, I snap myself." He demonstrated for her, pulling the rubber band back an inch or two and then letting go, feeling his raw skin sting again.

The girl's lips turned down and she nodded her head, as though digesting whether his story was believable or not, and deciding that it was.

"So, you're coming back then?" she asked, and he nodded. "Where from?"

"Iraq," he said simply. Not even his own mother had known the exact city.

"Did you kill anyone?"

His head snapped to the left and he stared down at her sternly. The words were so bare, so naked in their simplicity, it was almost as if he'd imagined them. The girl could have been asking him if it was hot in the desert.

"What?"

"I'm just wondering. It's a part of war. So...did you?"

"No," he lied smoothly, turning his face forward again. "It was actually pretty boring most of the time." He closed his eyes, but after only a second of peace, images of blood and pain flashed behind his eye- lids, so he opened them again.

"So, now that you're back, what college are you going to? That's what happens next for you, right?"

He turned his face to her again, surprised at the presumption. "What makes you think I'm going to school? I'm a soldier, not a scholar." He gestured at his uniform, which she was apparently impervious to.

"Oh, please," she replied, looking vaguely insulted. "You're not a lifetime soldier." When he looked bewildered, she plunged on. "First, you lie and lead me to believe that it wasn't totally crappy over there in that godforsaken desert, and then your eyes get all defensive. You're reading a well-worn copy of *Slaughterhouse Five,* so you're not a dummy. And your bookmark is a picture of a pretty girl I'm assuming you left back home. You love her. I can tell by how often you keep turning to look at it. So you clearly had other options. You took the Army route because it pays for college, something the parents couldn't afford, and maybe your jock scholarship fell through. I had you figured out before you had your seatbelt buckled. I'm just wondering what school the government will be paying you to attend."

Joel felt his brow furrow, and he bristled at her wild assumptions. He'd been in a company with plenty of other young men who were pretty smart and had other 'options,' but had foregone them. His officers were the same way. Sometimes you just choose to be a solder. Or it's something you're meant to do. This girl was so far out of line to assume that he wasn't one of those, however much she might be correct. He had indeed chosen not to re-enlist, a decision made so recently not even his parents or Kristen knew. They were expecting to welcome him home for a visit, and he couldn't wait to see their faces when he told them the truth.

His seatmate watched on in amusement as his face registered defensive irritation and then faded to concession. She'd judged him at first sight, and unlike his quick assessment of her, she was right on the money. Her perceptive manner had been highly unexpected when he'd labeled her as a freak. Freaks didn't have such laser-sharp intuition.

"The University of Texas," he said eventually, an air of resignation in his tone.

Her face lit up with a smug smile. "Majoring in...."

"I want to be a large animal vet," he said slowly, thinking of his horses back on the farm in Boonesville, Texas. He missed them almost as much as his missed Kristen. The weather report had been favorable for the weekend, and he couldn't wait to get back in the saddle. Literally.

The girl's face was confused. "Large animals like what? Polar Bears?"

He laughed, and it felt good to do so. "No, like horses."

"Oh," she said, cringing slightly. "I don't like horses."

"Nobody dislikes horses," he rebutted, trying in vain to think of anyone in Boonesville that would disagree with this.

"Well, I don't. They're too tall. I'm scared of heights."

Joel laughed again. He'd rappelled down a hundred feet from a moving helicopter before. The five or six foot fall from a horse was the least frightening thing he could imagine. And then her words took on a different meaning.

"You do realize that we're...um....flying right now?"

The girl closed her eyes and turned away from him. "Yes, soldier, I do. Why do you think I've been chatting at you? You're distracting me."

Joel smiled. "Well, then, perhaps it's my turn to ask irritating questions."

She grinned, still keeping her eyes closed. "Shoot."

"So what are you doing once you get to Dallas?"

"Nothing," she replied. "Changing planes."

"Where are you going then?"

"Kansas City. I'm going to the Paramore concert."

"To the what concert?"

She turned to face him, her oddly colored eyes turning a purplish shade of bewilderment. "Oh, come on! Paramore? The greatest female-fronted rock band in the history of forever?" When he still looked perplexed, she reached for the bag at her feet. "You've been off the continent too long, sir."

He watched on as she dragged a heavy looking canvas satchel into her lap. It was black, of course, but decorated with handwritten lyrics and cartoons in what looked like a white-out pen. She emerged a moment later with an mp3 player, which she switched on quickly and cued up, handing him one of the earphones.

They leaned close together and listened. The lyrics were a bit angry for Joel's taste; he had been raised on classic country and Baptist hymns. The girl was singing something about putting all of her faith in a boy, only to have him cast her aside. It reminded him uncomfortably of a fight he'd had with Kristen when he'd enlisted in the Army, but the singer's voice was pretty – powerful, while still remaining young and vulnerable.

He looked over at his neighbor, whose eyes were closed again. Her lips were moving along with the words, and a crease had formed between her eyes. She nodded in time to the driving beat, looking as though she were in deep prayer. The angst-heavy lyrics moved her deeply, like pages stolen from her own personal diary.

Joel grinned as he handed the earphone back to her. He could still hear the beat in his head and made a mental note to pick the CD up the next time he found himself in a Wal-Mart – another novelty he'd missed while hiking through the fiery sand.

"Great, right?" the girl asked, beaming.

"Yes, ma'am," he replied, pleased that he hadn't needed to lie.

"Ugh, don't call me ma'am. It's creepy." She reached her hand out. "I'm Charity," she said, grinning.

Joel took her hand, smirking. Half an hour ago, he wouldn't have been able to imagine a person less worthy of the name Charity. But she was just one of those books whose cover is incredibly misleading. He gave another smile as he looked down at her fingernails, which were very short for a girl's, though pained with shiny black polish. "I'm Joel," he said.

Just then the plan dipped a few feet, responding to a rogue pocket of air. Charity gripped Joel's hand fiercely, slamming her eyes shut and sucking in a sharp breath. She uttered a rather vicious curse word, and Joel laughed.

"Maybe you need a swear bracelet, too." He pried his fingers out of hers and patted the back of her hand gently. She had yet to reopen her eyes, though she'd given a little smirk at his attempt at a joke.

"I just need to keep talking," she said decidedly. "Tell me about your girl, the one in the picture you keep staring at."

"Kristen," he said fondly, feeling the way he said her name like a prayer.

Charity leaned back in the seat, forcing her body into a calmer posture. "How did you two meet?"

Joel thought back. "I can't even remember. We were probably in strollers next to each other. We grew up together. She was my high school sweetheart. Love of my life."

"Let me see the picture again," Charity mumbled, breathing deeply and fighting to relax over the little tremors of turbulence that continued to shake the plane. Joel obliged, letting her see the photo- graph that had been taken last year at his farm. By some miracle, it had come out looking almost professional. The sun was pushing through her dark hair, turning it nearly auburn, and little sunspots gleamed from her eyelashes and across her smile. She was breathtaking. Even Charity, whose conceptions of beauty seemed a bit skewed, was forced to con- cede. "She's pretty. Let me guess....cheerleader?"

Perceptive as always. "Yes," Joel admitted.

"And you were a jock, I assume." She looked him up and down once as though deciding which sport better fit his body. "Football? No wait, you were reading baseball scores earlier." Her eyes missed nothing.

"Both, actually. I'm from a small town. You can play every sport there is if you have the stamina to go to all the practices." He preferred baseball, truly. The sport carried less prestige than football in Texas perhaps, but it hurt a heck of a lot less. And he hated seeing the worry on Kristen's face on Friday nights when he limped away from a vicious tackle.

"So, I was right about the sport scholarship?"

Joel gave a bitter laugh. "As it turns out, being the best corner- back in Boonesville, Texas earned me fourth string for the Longhorns. I would never have taken the field on a Saturday. And though you were right about me not being dumb, I'm not exactly much of a student. The little bit of scholarship money I got for my academics didn't make a dent in the tuition. I'd nearly bankrupted my parents after the first semester. So, I found a recruiter and enlisted."

"You don't love it though." She didn't ask this; she just said it like it was fact.

"What's to love?" he muttered, feeling strangely at ease admit- ting this. He'd never before hinted that serving his country wasn't the ultimate achievement. "It's overcrowded on base, and yet you're always alone. You get homesick, and then you just get sick. The food is crap, and the hours are terrible. You get to build your muscles up and play with weapons, but then they ship you over to this foreign planet that feels it was built on the sun. And then....it's not play anymore. Everything is real, and yet nothing feels real at all. It feels like this hot, sweaty dream that never seems to end."

Joel turned to see that Charity's eyes were wide with surprise. He cringed, realizing how dumb his rant would sound to a stranger. It would sound dumb to pretty much anyone.

"Sorry. That was lame of me to just babble on like that. Maybe I need a bracelet for when I talk too much." He smirked and gave himself another snap with the rubber band.

Charity punched him on the arm. "Quit it," she said with a smirk. "I asked you to talk to me. And you shouldn't feel ashamed of what you feel."

Joel frowned, not wanting this to get all serious. He wanted to focus on going home to Kristen. Maybe he'd go home first and ask his parents for a loan. Then he could buy Kristen the ring she wanted, and they could get started on all of their dreams.

But when he thought of those dreams, he could only see how he'd put them on hold to serve his country. He could only see the hurt in Kristen's eyes when he'd explained how many more years it would take before they could get married and start a family. And then there was the numb horror in her eyes when Joel had been deployed. She hadn't cried. She hadn't screamed or thrown anything or stormed out. She'd just been frozen, her emotions locking her into place.

Joel frowned again, and Charity gave him another whack on the arm. "Are you beating yourself up mentally, soldier? It's not good for you. Keep talking to me....remember, I'm a very nervous flier and you're the type that can't keep from helping a woman in need."

He cut his eyes over to her and she was grinning faintly. He could see the shred of fear in her eyes still, but it was clear that he was the one in need between the two of them. He sat back heavily in his seat, feeling his eyes finally begin to burn from tiredness. It had been ages since he'd slept properly.

"We don't have to talk about Iraq," she continued. "We can talk about anything. Tell me about your home and your horses."

Joel smiled, and began to prattle on about his white mare named Shadow and his big black gelding named Faust. He tried his best to ignore the twist of disgust on Charity's face when he mentioned how he loved to take Shadow for a blazing gallop through his parents' acreage. No matter how he explained the thrill of all that big wind in his face and all that powerful animal underneath him, he couldn't get her to budge on the issue. "Not even a little trot?"

"Drop it, soldier," she replied tightly, and he help up his hands in surrender.

"Well, aside from going out of state for concerts, what do you like to do?" he asked, stretching and feeling the bliss of relaxation finally stealing over his body.

"I read," she said, and it was one of the least surprising things she'd uttered since they'd met. He'd seen a slew of books in her satchel when she'd dug it out earlier, but he would have pegged her for a prolific reader anyway. Especially after she'd opened her mouth and started handing out five-dollar words.

"And what are you reading right now?" he asked, trying to draw a bit more out of her. As much as he didn't really want to admit it, he enjoyed talking with her.

"*Slaughterhouse Five,*" she replied tightly. The plane had gone back to jostling just a bit, which was plenty for Charity's nerves.

Joel chuckled at her joke. "Seriously."

"Well, I've emptied the bookstore's selection of angsty teen novels, so I moved on to the classics. I'm reading *The Picture of Dorian Gray.*"

Joel raised his eyebrows. It was such a classic that he'd never heard of it, not that he would ever doubt her about such things.

She seemed irritated that he wasn't following, however. "Oscar Wilde?" Her face was lit up and she didn't seem to register the next few hiccups in the planes' trajectory.

"Oh, I've heard of him," Joel said, wracking his brain. "Isn't he the gay one?"

Charity gave a sharp intake of breath, a wicked gleam appearing in her strangely colored eyes. "Oh, is that all you know about him? Wonderful. Do we get to have a scintillating debate about gays in the military now? Please say yes!"

The businessman on the aisle, who had shot them confused looks now and again, shifted uncomfortably in his seat and stared determinedly at his laptop. Joel rolled his eyes hugely. "No, we are not. I'm certainly sorry I brought it up."

Charity pretended to be incredibly disappointed. "It would have been a good debate, I bet."

Joel answered with a laugh. He didn't doubt that in the slight- est. Intent on corralling this conversation, he turned to face the seatback ahead of him, nestling into the seat. "When you're not reading, what else do you do?"

"Um," she replied, picking at a fingernail. "I don't know. I write, I guess."

"Poems about death and pain?" he jabbed, chuckling.

"Good Lord, Joel, you might be the most stereotypical person I've ever met!"

He closed his eyes, feeling the lovely sensation of calm even as he laughed with his neighbor. "I'm just giving you a hard time. But you have to understand that your...*look* affects the way people see you. It's no different than my uniform."

"People see your uniform as a sign of heroism and bravery. They see my clothes as a sign that I'm some delinquent that's depressed all the time and thinks about suicide."

"So, why do you dress like that?" he asked, still keeping his eyes closed. The questions were coming slower as something like sleep threatened on the horizon.

"I'm expressing myself. I'm being an individual." It was her standard reply, and he could tell that she knew it wasn't ringing true just now.

"By dressing like everyone else your age? Yeah, that's so brave and unique of you." He gave another chuckle, retreating into the dark- ness behind his eyelids.

When she replied, her voice was softer and more thoughtful. Though he didn't look, he imagined her brow was furrowed in concentration as she took the billions of words she'd read and the words she'd written, trying to arrange them into a pattern that fit this question perfectly. "I started dressing like this because I was rebelling against my parents. I kept dressing this way because people leave me alone. They give me a wide berth, and I like it that way. I don't really like talking to people."

"Could have fooled me," Joel said, his words slurring out on the edge of sleep. Peace was maybe thirty seconds away. As it was, Charity's reply was lost in the fog, her words turning into marshmallow clouds.

But something was wrong. Those clouds were familiar, and be- fore Joel could blink himself awake, he was stuck back in the place he hated most lately: his nightmare. It was that same day, of course it was. The clouds were so puffy and innocuous, no one would have expected anything to go wrong.

He was in the second of three Humvees in their convoy, running the same strip of sand that they ran three times a week. Joel was to the point where he could recognize the shrubs and other scrubby bushes that lined the roadway. He was bored. And so was Pete. Joel hadn't known Pete until their tour here. Pete was the top bunk and Joel was the bottom. When Pete started to snore in the night, Joel would kick under his mat- tress. When Joel would moan and whine about Kristen too much, Pete would punch him or hide his picture of her. They were friends. They wouldn't have been close had they grown up together perhaps, but none of that mattered in the sandbox.

Joel shifted in the dream. He knew all of this had already happened, and no matter what he did now, it couldn't be changed. But he would try. He always tried. He turned to Pete. Pete's eyes were the same color as the sky that supported those marshmallow clouds.

"Pete, don't get out of the truck." Joel had a hand on Pete's arm. "No matter what, okay buddy? Stay here!"

"You worry too much, Joel," was Pete's reply. That was always his reply. Joel swore, and then reached for his bracelet, but there was nothing there. He hadn't started wearing it yet. No point. He swore again.

That's when the gunfire began. The first rounds took out the truck behind them. The heat from the fireball was intense. Joel had for- gotten that things could be hotter than the Iraqi sun. The second set of rounds missed destroying any vehicles, but the driver of the first Humvee was clearly dead when the smoke cleared. The truck began to drive off the sandy road as the other soldiers in it tried to regain control of the situation.

"Don't do it Pete," Joel whispered as Pete turned his sky-bright eyes on him.

"I'm gonna jog up there and make sure everything's alright," Pete announced, leaping out without another word.

"Of course you are," Joel replied tiredly. This is the part where he began pinching his skin, punching the dashboard, anything to wake up, to get out of here. It never worked, but he would never, ever stop trying. Even something as simple as keeping his eyes closed was forbidden here. He would have to watch every second in high-resolution.

Pete wasn't ten feet in front of the truck when the shot hit him. Some vicious high-caliber round that was designed to shred him from the inside once it penetrated the skin. The force of the impact shot him back to where he collided with Joel's truck, taking half of his body through the windshield. Joel prayed for the thousandth time just for the ability to close his eyes. But instead, he saw his friend, drenched in red, his chest smoking from the heat of the bullet. He saw the sky-colored eyes blink rapidly and then stop. And he saw the last liquid breath of the guy who shared a bunk with him at their camp.

Something sharp was stinging his left wrist, and suddenly he was soaring upward through the puffy clouds and landing with a jerk in seat 19F of an airplane bound for Dallas. Charity was leaning over him anxiously, her fingers pulling back on his rubber band bracelet, poising for another snap.

"What?" Joel asked with a groggy voice.

"You were swearing in your sleep," she chastised. "Rather fluently, actually. Dude next to me was getting nervous. And making people nervous on a plane isn't a smart play, soldier."

"I'll keep that in mind," he snapped acidly. He could see that his tone hurt her feelings, but was too raw to care.

"Fine, fine. Go on back to your little post-traumatic stress dream you were having there," she said tightly. "But you should know we'll be landing soon." She turned away from him with a huff, but not before snapping him once more with the rubber band.

Joel stretched. He'd slept longer than he'd thought, longer than he should have, which was not at all. Charity had a valid point about exposing his crazy sleep-taking nightmares to strangers on an airplane. And if they were landing soon, he didn't want bad blood between then. Though they had only just met, Joel found her opinion of him very important for some reason.

"Listen, Charity, sorry I snapped at you there. You were right about the bad dream." He gave a shrug. "I wanted to thank you. You made this plane trip a thousand times more interesting than it could have been." He gave his most winning smile and she returned it with a sarcastic grin.

"Alright, alright. You helped me out, too. Without you here to talk to, I would be chatting *this* guy's ear off. And I can't imagine he'd be as nice as you about it." She jabbed her thumb in the direction of the businessman on the aisle, who couldn't hide behind his laptop any longer. He gave a wince that he was even being discussed by such a scary girl, and seemed a bit too fascinated by the back of the seat in front of him.

Joel gave a rousing laugh as the plane touched down and Charity seemed surprised. "Normally I throw up right before the landing," she mused, and Joel made a face at her, but still kept a healthy distance in case her nausea was delayed.

They filed out into the terminal and reached the hallway where Joel would head toward baggage claim and Charity would go find her connecting flight to Kansas City. They paused, searching for appropriate parting words. As the seconds passed, Joel noticed that people were making strange faces at the two of them together. He smiled at the fact that he had the pleasure of knowing the girl under the scary clothes and makeup. At least a little bit.

"Enjoy your concert," he said, and she nodded, looking just as hesitant to part ways.

"Enjoy your girl. You should marry her. Well, you should ask her, at least." She smiled at him.

"I think I will," he said with a grin. They were moving apart now, waving as they stepped backwards into the flow of traffic.

"I hope you find some new angsty teen books to read," he called.

"I hope you don't fall off your horse!" She had to yell to be heard.

He laughed, and when he turned, her dark head had vanished into the sea of commuters. Turning back, he broke into a run, more anxious than ever to fall into the arms of the girl he loved. And because of his uniform, the crowds parted easily to let him pass.

BOARDING PASS

PASSENGER RECEIPT 1 OF 1

Miller, Jean

Miller, Jean

DFW — STL

Chapter Five

Global Air

SEAT NUMBER

19F

Date and Time
JUNE 09, 2017
04:00 PM

Destination: STL

Chapter Five

DFW to STL (Jean)

What a lousy way to spend her 50th birthday. Instead of celebrating a successful job interview in Dallas, Jean found herself jammed into the window seat on a crowded and delayed flight back to St. Louis, sweltering in the 105 degree Texas heat. Her black pinstriped interview suit clung to her sweaty body in a most uncomfortable manner, and her feet were swollen and tired.

Jean had been feeling that her life was at a crossroads for quite a while now. Seventeen years as a travelling pharmaceutical sales rep had left her tired and discouraged. She was often on the road 15-20 days per month, and spent more time in airports and hotel rooms than in her own small apartment. This hectic travel schedule had been hard on her relationships – she could barely keep her houseplants alive, much less cultivate friendships or find a boyfriend. Whenever she WAS at home, it was usually only long enough to do laundry, pay a few bills, and repack her suitcase for another week or two of travel.

So when she had heard of an opportunity in Dallas to advance her career while spending less time on the road, she thought it would be a perfect way to start her life over. This promotion would afford her the opportunity to settle down into a routine where she would make friends and even join a church. Over the past few weeks she had sailed through two rounds of phone interviews and was excited to be one of final three candidates invited to the headquarters in Dallas for product testing and a tour of the corporate office. Who could have guessed it would turn out so badly? From the moment she walked in the door early that morning, she knew taking this job would be a huge mistake. The people were rude and the corporate culture was hostile and intimidating. The interview did not go all that well, and Jean felt that about half way through she must have said the wrong thing, because she could feel the air go out of the room. They took her to a testing area and told her she had as much time as she needed to take the online test. The test was very complex, and everyone knew it was going to take several hours to complete. But every half-hour or so, the secretary would interrupt her and ask if she had completed the test because they wanted to call a taxi to take her back to the airport. When lunch time came around, they acted annoyed to have to go to Subway to get her a sandwich. She finally quit the test early, knowing that she did not finish and would get penalized. But she was certain that she did not want the job anyway – in fact, she could not get out the door fast enough. The taxi took her to the airport and she rushed to the check-in counter to see if she could fly standby on an earlier flight. Her frequent flyer status helped her get one of the last available seats on this flight, and even though she preferred to fly in business class, she rushed down the jet bridge and sank exhaustedly near the window, in seat 19F. She hated sitting next to the window, often feeling trapped into a small space by strangers who may or may not let her up to stretch her legs or go to the restroom. Ironically, this was much the same way she felt trapped by her life and a lifetime of questionable decisions.

"I am sorry Miss Miller," the ticket agent had told her, "but the best seat available is 19F."

"Nothing else?" Jean asked dejectedly. "I have tons of airline miles I will gladly give you if you can find anything else."

"No, nothing in Business Class or even on the aisle. Just a few window seats and a dozen or so in the middle."

"OK, I guess it's 19F for me. No offense, but I just really want out of Dallas ASAP."

The plane continued to fill and Jean watched in dismay as family after family joined her in the crowded airliner. Everyone seemed to be going on vacation, and were taking huge carry-on bags with them. As a seasoned road warrior, Jean carried virtually nothing with her onto the plane. Do these people not understand that space is limited in the overhead bins? Somewhere behind her a baby started to wail, and Jean's mood sank even further. This was going to be a long flight for sure.

Finally everyone was on board, including an elderly couple who sat down in the aisle and middle seats next to her. They struggled with their seatbelts and the wife wanted to hold her giant purse in her lap in- stead of putting it under the seat in front of her. The husband, who was seated next to the aisle, was having trouble getting settled and it was obvious that neither had flown in quite some time. They studied the safety information card and looked for the nearest exit. All Jean wanted to do was to get home and cool off – why was this plane so hot? She adjusted the air vent above her, but nothing but warm air was pumping out. Soon the flight attendant made the announcement that Jean had been dreading....there was an electrical problem with the air conditioning, but the mechanics were working on it and they hoped to be in the air within 30 minutes. The plane had been heating up while sitting on the tarmac in the hot Dallas sun, and was getting warmer by the minute. Jean struggled out of her suit jacket as sweat started to trickle slowly down her back. She saw her flushed reflection in the window, and was saddened at how tired she looked. Her once flaming red hear was starting to gray, especially around her face. The same thing had happened to her mother, but her dad had loved it, calling it her "halo." Jean felt her halo drooping a bit today, and there were dark circles under her pale blue eyes, along with frown lines on her brow. Beads of perspiration glistened on her forehead and cheeks, and a ring was pooling at the base of her neck.

Jean grabbed the safety information card from the seat pocket in front of her – after all the flights she had been on, she had it memorized, but knew it was sturdy and would make a good fan. While waving it back and forth with her left hand, she picked up the in-flight magazine with her right. Realizing she had thoroughly read it during her flight to Dallas yesterday afternoon, she started to put it back. Her eye noticed something sticking out of the magazine - it was a boarding pass for someone named Lisa Davis who had been in this seat on a flight from Des Moines to Chicago earlier this morning. Also folded neatly in the bottom of the seat pocket was a *Des Moines Register* from this morning, open to the sports section.

The small child seated behind Jean was getting restless and started kicking the back of her seat. Jean began to think about Lisa Davis – "Who was she and why had she been in this seat? Where was she going so early this morning? Is her life any more fulfilling than mine? Did she spend her 50th birthday jammed into a crowded plane full of strangers, or did she celebrate with friends and family?" Jean's mood continued to deteriorate as the child behind her climbed up the back of her seat and pulled her hair. She shot a stern glare back toward the child's mother, but the mom was busy reading a book and did not notice. Soon the child started to cry in earnest and Jean closed her eyes in exhaustion. She listened to the couple next to her fretting about the delay.

"George, what are we going to do if we miss the connection in St. Louis?" the wife asked, almost in tears. "You know how important this trip is!"

Finally the air conditioning was fixed, and the plane pushed back from the gate. Jean checked her watch and found that they were leaving nearly 45 minutes late – almost the exact time she would be boarding her originally scheduled flight where she would have been flying Business Class in an aisle seat and with working air conditioning. So much for her brilliant idea of flying standby and getting home earlier. The flight attendants made their usual safety speech, and Jean found herself quoting it along with them in her head. The elderly man and wife next to her nervously followed every word, and were concerned about turning their seat cushions into flotation devices. They were obviously fearful of flying and wondered how to work the oxygen masks. In all of Jean's travels, she had never needed a flotation device or an oxygen mask. But there was always a first time for everything, she guessed. Just not today, please God, not today.

Jean stared out of the window and reflected back over the past several years. Her small Illinois family became even smaller when both of her parents passed away last summer – first Mom from cancer and then Dad just a few months later from heart failure (and probably a bro- ken heart as well). They had been married one week short of 59 years when Mom succumbed to her breast cancer. Jean glanced down at her wrist to the pink bracelet she wore in her Mom's honor, and said a short prayer. One of the few commitments Jean was able to make the past few years was participating in the *Komen Walk for the Cure*. But losing both of her parents back-to-back like that had left Jean feeling pretty lost and lonely.

She was not very close to her two older brothers Mike and Tom, or to her much younger sister Liz. They were all married and had kids and grandkids of their own. Never having married or even seriously dated, she usually felt out of place at family gatherings. Perhaps that is why she chose a life on the road – it was less painful to be lonely in a hotel room in a strange town than at home where she could see everyone else so happy. This past Christmas had been particularly difficult, since it was the first one since their parents' deaths. They had all gathered at Liz's home on Christmas day, and the grandkids spent the day playing with new toys and video games. But it was painfully obvious that there were two empty chairs at the dinner table, and Jean found that she did not have much of an appetite.

After taxiing around DFW for another fifteen minutes or so, the plane took its place in line, waiting to take off. The captain announced that they were 10th in line and Jean watched as the planes ahead of her took off to places unknown. She could not help but wonder where they were going, and if their air conditioning worked betters than hers did. Finally they were in the air, and plane began to cool a bit. Jean rested her head against the window and tried to ignore the screaming children behind her, while wondering what to do with her life when she got home. After about half an hour in the air, the child behind her had finally cried himself to sleep, and Jean was trying to drift off to sleep as well. Suddenly, there was a commotion beside her as the woman next to her decided she needed to get something out of her bag that was in the overhead bin. Jean used this chance to climb out into the aisle and head to the back of the plane to stretch her legs. Even thought she was barely five feet tall, Jean found the confines of a window seat quite confining indeed. Plus, she had read somewhere about the dangers of blood clots in the legs if you sit too long. She spent the next few minutes pacing the aisle, trying to ease her troubled spirit as well as her cramped muscles. She got a cup of ice water from one of the flight attendants, and studied her 100+ fellow passengers who were in various stages of flight fatigue. She knew that feeling all too well.

She overheard the flight attendants discussing the usually long day their aircraft was having. Usually, a plane of this size would make five or six flights in a 24-hour day. However, the NTSB had found a defect in the landing gear of several planes, and a huge portion of the fleet had been grounded. This plane was one that had been called to pick up the slack, increasing the number of flights to eight today. Jean hoped the old bird was up to the task, and that they could land safely. She really was not in the mood for any more excitement.

After a few minutes, she returned to her seat and looked for something interesting to read. The airplane took an unexpected lurch as it hit a bit of turbulence, and the older woman next to her let out a gasp. Jean instinctively turned to her and said, "It'll be OK, just a bit of bumpiness here and there. No cause for alarm."

"You travel a lot?" the woman asked nervously.

"Yes, almost every week. Have been doing it for years. This is nothing to get worried about, trust me."

"You really fly EVERY week? For business? This is the first time we have flown since 9/11 – things sure have changed!"

"Yes, 9/11 changed everything for all of us. I'm a pharmaceutical sales rep, and travel to different hospitals and physician clinics all across the country. I've been doing it for so long I hardly remember doing anything else."

"Wow, that sounds so exciting. My husband George and I are retired now, and usually the only travel we do is with our RV. But we are on our way to our grandson Peter's college graduation in Michigan. We have five children and 12 grandchildren – have not missed a graduation yet!"

"Well, that's pretty amazing, too. Sounds like you guys keep busy. I don't have any kids, but lots of nieces and nephews. I don't make it to many graduations, though."

"Oh, but I'm sure you go to so many exciting places and see so many wonderful things."

"Actually, most of what I see are airport terminals and hotel rooms. I spend most of my time working or writing reports until late at night. I really don't get much time to go sightseeing."

"Oh, that's too bad. You should take some time off for yourself and actually see this wonderful country of ours!"

Jean returned to her task of finding something to read. Unfolding the *Register* from the seat pocket, she quickly dismissed the sports news and headed instead to the human interest stories. Not finding these rural Iowans very interesting, she tried the employment section instead. "Maybe I should give Iowa a try?" she thought. "St. Louis is sure not working out for me." She turned the page and was amused to find a story about starting a new career as a *mature* adult (over 50). Well, she qualified for that as of today, so she read suggestions from employment specialists and HR executives. They stressed the need to work with a passion, doing what you love. One section in particular seemed written just for her:

"Another thing that older workers struggle with these days is the fact that they are working longer and postposing retirement until age 70 or later. Gone are the days of working at one job until age 62 or 65 and then sitting on the porch in a rocking chair, living off a corporate pension. Most baby-boomers have changed not only employers but whole careers numerous times by age 55, and are feeling burned out and burned up. They worry about the economy and the fear that they have not saved enough for retirement. Many are concerned about dragging through their final work years in jobs that offer little satisfaction or fulfillment. The trick is to find something that will not only pay the bills but offer these experienced workers a chance to make a contribution and feel valued by the organization. And if they can also be doing a job they love, all the better!"

She tore the article from the newspaper and returned the rest of the paper to the seat pocket. She read the article again and again, trying to re-evaluate her goals and ambitions. She knew she was tired of the constant air travel, but what should she do with her life? She still had almost 20 years to work before she could retire, and needed to make as much money as possible to fund her golden years. As a single female with no children, she was facing those golden years alone, and right now they were not looking so shiny.

She closed her weary eyes and tried to envision what the "perfect" life for her would look like. Sadly, she just kept coming up with mostly questions and few answers. The article said that she should do what she loved, but what is that? What would it feel like to have a job she actually enjoyed going to each day? Having something that she felt passionate about, instead of something that just paid the bills? Having a job with a regular schedule so that she could actually plan time with family and friends? Actually having friends?

She folded the article to put it into her purse, but noticed a picture on the reverse side. It was an advertisement for a local TV talk show telling of a middle-aged Iowa woman who self-published a book that had become the newest literary sensation. It had been on top of the *New York Times* best seller list for several weeks and had gotten rave reviews. The author was to be on the local talk show next week to tell of her journey from school secretary to successful author. She had written the book in her spare time at home, and did not have an agent or publishing firm backing her. She had found a way to self-publish the book, and printed only a few copies at a time. She gave a few away as gifts, but urged everyone she knew to order the books online – she even had an electronic version and was considering an audio book! She used social media to promote the book, and eventually word got around. The rest was history!

Jean thought about how much she used to enjoy writing, and how her friends and teachers always said she had potential for a great novel. She had tinkered around with it a bit as a college student, working on the school newspaper and entering poetry contests. With all of her recent travels, she certainly had enough material to write something interesting. Pulling a scrap of paper and a pen from her purse, she started to jot down a few ideas. She had been to 47 of the 50 states, and even to Europe twice. She had flown on hundreds of flights over the years and met thousands of people. What kind of story could she write? Romance? Mystery? Thriller? And where should it be set? California? New Hampshire? Italy? The ideas started tumbling around in her head and out onto the paper. She was so focused on writing that she no longer heard the crying babies or felt the heat and claustrophobia of the crowded airplane. She glanced again at the boarding pass for Lisa Davis and again wondered about her life. She turned the small piece of paper over and over in her hands, almost willing it to tell Lisa's story. She quickly lost all track of time, and the next thing she knew they were taxiing to the gate in St. Louis. She tucked the boarding pass and her notes into a pocket of her small carry-on, thanked the pilot for a safe flight (as she always did), and headed to the gate area. There was quite a crowd of people waiting to board the plane (since the flight had arrived almost an hour late) and she almost tripped over a young boy sitting on the floor listening to his IPod.

Finally in the main terminal, she passed a newsstand and glanced at the books for sale. Perhaps she would see HER book there someday! With the first smile to grace her face in quite some time, Jean's pace quickened as she headed toward baggage claim and then into the summer afternoon heat.

Happy Birthday, Jean!

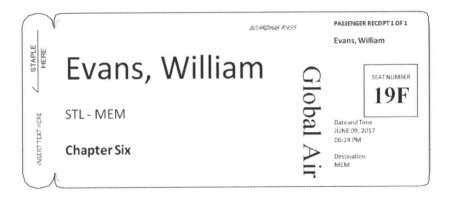

BOARDING PASS

Evans, William

STL - MEM

Chapter Six

Global Air

PASSENGER RECEIPT 1 OF 1

Evans, William

SEAT NUMBER
19F

Date and Time
JUNE 09, 2017
06:24 PM

Destination
MEM

Chapter Six

STL to MEM (Will)

Was there any possible way to make it more obvious to everyone in the airport that he was an unaccompanied minor? Will Evans stared in dismay at the large blue plastic pouch hanging around his neck. His mother had just left him in the care of a flight attendant to be escorted down the jet bridge for his short flight to see his dad in Memphis. He was only a few weeks short of his 10th birthday, but to this stupid airline, he was still too young to fly without an escort. Good grief! Because he had gone with his mom on several of her business trips, he'd been on more airplane flights than many of the people in this place, but rules were rules, and everyone continued to treat him like a baby. He even had to wait next to the gate and be MONITORED by some old lady who insisted on hovering over him. The incoming flight had been delayed – again– and in frustration, he flopped down next to the wall and pulled out his IPOD. He closed his eyes to listen to the angry rap music that seemed to be such a big part of his life these days.

Will was tall for his age, slender and long-legged. His mother complained that he could grow an inch in his sleep, making his jeans too short overnight. His pale eyes and slender face were framed by a mop of curly brown hair. He was wearing a Superman t-shirt and his long legs were stretched out in front of him. He kept a nervous hand on his backpack – not wanting to take the chance of losing it.

The flight attendant firmly shook his shoulder and said that the incoming flight was finally about to reach the gate. From the look on her face, he could tell she had been calling his name for a while. Obviously, the sound had gotten lost behind the thud of the bass in his ears.

The gate agent announced the arrival of the flight from Dallas and once everyone was finally off, the old lady escorted him down the jet bridge to the plane. They stopped at the door of the plane, and Will was formally handed off to the flight attendants on board. They checked his paperwork again, and a young girl in her early 20's escorted him down the aisle to his seat. He kicked his small backpack under the seat in front of him and fastened his seatbelt.

Officially in his place next to the window in seat 19F, Will watched as the baggage handlers loaded the suitcases into the cargo area of the plane. He was always fascinated by the inner workings of the airport, and how they could keep all of the bags on the right planes. He often thought he would love to work in aviation somehow. Relieved to see his Memphis Grizzlies duffle bag on the conveyer belt, he relaxed a bit. Nothing would be worse than a long weekend with his dad and not having his own stuff. This visit was going to be bad enough without losing his luggage as well. Plus, his dad had sent that bag to him for Christmas a few years back, and it meant a lot to him.

His mom and dad had been divorced almost five years now, after another five years of friction and discontent. Will could not remember a time when they had been a happy family. After the divorce, Will and his mom had left Memphis and moved to St. Louis to be closer to his maternal grandparents. He could count on one hand the number of times he had seen his dad since then. Out of sight, out of mind, as the saying goes. So when his mom told him that an email from his dad had arrived a week ago, Will was shocked, but secretly excited. Then he read the email, and could barely contain his anger and disappointment. His dad wanted him to come for a visit now that school was out for the summer, but not because he missed him and wanted to spend time with him. NO, he wanted Will to meet his new wife and three new step-children.

The other passengers started to board and plane, and Will silently said a prayer for the seat next to him to remain vacant. He really did not want anyone that near to him right now. Much to his dismay, an older Hispanic woman sat in the seat next to the aisle, and gave him a curious glance. Her hair was completely gray and in a way it reminded him of his own grandmother. "Is no one sitting here?" she asked as she pointed to the middle seat. "Are you alone?" She seemed genuinely concerned, but Will was not in the mood.

"No, no one is sitting there, and yes, I am alone," Will answered, trying hard to be polite but barely hiding his frustration. He pointed to the 'unaccompanied minor' badge around his neck and then turned back to the window.

"Oh, dear, I'm sorry you have to travel alone," the woman gushed. "I just hate to see young folks flying by themselves – so many things can go wrong! I certainly hope whoever is picking you up on the other end knows we have been delayed almost an hour already."

"Yes, ma'am," Will answered sweetly, while uttering a few choice words under his breath. "My dad knows we'll be late."

"Oh, I feel so bad for young kids growing up without their dads. Such a sad sign of the times, I guess."

Will really did not want to get into this conversation with a strange person. He was trying hard to keep these feelings buried, where they had less power over him. Turning away from the woman to hide the slight tear that was fighting to slip from his eye, he pretended to be interested in the other planes outside his window. That woman had no idea how hard it has been for him without his dad.

Will had enormous respect for his mother and how hard she worked to provide for them during the past five years. He was old enough now to understand the fatigue in her voice at the end of her 10- hour shifts at the local casino where she worked in the back office. She also traveled to other casinos in the Midwest for training. She was taking online classes at night, studying business management and hoping to climb the ladder at work. Will came home from school each afternoon to an empty apartment, but his grandparents lived just down the street so he often went there instead. Grandma always fed him a snack and helped him with his homework. Sometimes when his mom came to pick him up, they would stay for dinner as well. Grandma seemed to know when they both needed a little extra attention. Just last night she had fixed his favorite dinner of spaghetti and garlic bread. She and Grandpa were happy about this trip to see his dad.

"Will, I am so glad you have this chance to spend a few days with your dad," his grandma had said over dessert of angel food cake and strawberries, another of his favorites. "I know it will be a little strange having other people in your old house, but I'm sure you will be fine. And flying by yourself – wow! When did you get so grown up, young man?"

"So, what do you guys have planned?" his grandpa had asked between bites of cake.

"I'm not totally sure. Gonna get some good ribs, that's for sure!" Will really missed the Memphis barbeque. St. Louis ribs were fine, but not as good as what he used to eat as a little kid. "And there is a new 3-D Disney film at the IMAX that the girls want to see. Other than that, the weekend is fairly free, I think."

"Well, whatever you end up doing, I know it will be fun. Now, how about a game of skip-bo before you leave?"

Will knew that they meant well, but he could not help but be apprehensive about meeting his dad's new family. Was it really possible to stop caring about one family and start over with a new one?

He was just beginning to understand the friction between his parents, although his mother tried hard to hide it. His dad rarely called, and had visited only a couple of times since the divorce. He had gotten behind with his child support payments once, and the tension had really escalated then.

But now that he had been gone so long, Will and his mom had settled into a kind of strange routine where his dad was seldom mentioned.

But Will thought about him all the time. As much as he loved and respected his mother, he really missed having a dad around. When he was at the mall or church and saw boys his age sitting with their dads, he felt a pang of loss and jealousy. And he could not help but feel that dad's absence was somehow his fault. Had he done something wrong that would make his dad not care about him anymore? Maybe his dad would have paid more attention to him if he were smarter? More athletic? He knew that he looked a lot like his dad had when he was a young boy – a crooked smile and dimples that everyone thought were so cute. He had one family picture that had been taken the last Christmas they were all together before the divorce. He was fairly oblivious to the tensions then, but now he could easily see the stress on everyone's faces. He did remember the fights – the yelling and crying behind closed doors. Although they had tried to shield him, he knew something was wrong.

The captain came on the intercom to announce that the plane was ready to leave the gate. He apologized for the delay but said that he hoped they could "fly fast" and make up as much time as possible. Since the flight from St. Louis to Memphis was only scheduled to be about 40 minutes, and they had been delayed almost 60 minutes, just how fast was the pilot going to fly anyway? Will was not sure he wanted to know the answer, but he adjusted his seatbelt just to be safe.

The flight attendants gave their usual safety speech about oxy- gen masks and finding the nearest exit. Will wasn't crazy to be sitting so close to the rear of the airplane, but at least there was an exit back here if he needed it.

He pulled the wrinkled email from his dad out of his pocket and tried for the umpteenth time to read between the lines, to understand why his dad would contact him, now of all times.

Hey, Billy…I hope you are enjoying your summer. I have big news! I got married last month to a nice lady named Lily and she has three little girls:

Emma, Colby and Sophie. They have moved into the house and are busy getting settled in, but I would love for you to come for a few days to meet them. I'll have a ticket waiting if you can come next weekend – miss 'ya buddy. Love, Dad

Will had talked to his mom about it, and she did not want to keep him from going, if that was what he wanted to do.

"Of course you can go," his mom had told him. "If you want to, that is. This is totally your decision. Swimming lessons don't start for about a month, and the church camp-out is in August. Actually, this would be a good time. But it's up to you."

He had called dad later that night only to find out that two of the girls had moved into his old bedroom and already painted it princess pink. There was no place for him to sleep except for on an inflatable mattress on the floor of the office, and for some reason that really bugged him. Not that he expected his dad to keep his old room like it was in the old days, like some sort of shrine or something, but pink? Three little girls? He replaced me with three little girls? And it had been so long since they had talked, his dad did not even know that he went by the name "Will" now...no one called him Billy anymore!

The flight attendant stopped by to check on him and make sure he was securely buckled in. She then presented him with his "junior flight wings." Will carefully folded the email around the wing-shaped pin and slipped them into his pocket. As much as the words from the email frustrated him, it was one of the few communications he had from his dad, and in some strange way he wanted to protect it. He wondered how it will make him feel to see his dad with the new family, treating another woman nicer than he ever saw him treat his mom. And did he know more about these little girls than he did his own flesh-and-blood son?

Shortly after the plane took off, Will felt an intense pain in his left ear. Ever since a severe infection when he was seven, he had trouble with pressure building in his ear during flights. He reached into his backpack to pull out his favorite double-bubble chewing gum, and saw a strange envelope in a side pocket. Curious, he opened it to find a letter from his mom.

Hi, Will. By now you're on the plane and headed to your weekend with your dad. I just wanted to write a short note to let you know that I'm so proud of you and the fantastic young man you are becoming. I know that growing up without your dad in the house has been really hard on you, and I've seen you struggle with frustrations and loneliness that I have not been able to fix. As your mom, I've tried to shelter you from pain but also give you the wings to learn and grow and develop the amazing potential we all know you have.

Your dad and I were very young when we first got together, and since he had grown up without a dad of his own, I am not sure he really understood what it meant to be a father. I'm not making excuses, just trying to explain. I know you were really little when you dad and I separated, but I am sure you know that things had been rough between us. But he did love you – DOES love you – and I don't ever want you to forget that.

You know that he and I don't talk very often, but when I heard about the marriage and the three little girls, I was surprised, yet hopeful that he had finally gotten his priorities in order and was ready to settle down and be a family man. And the fact that he contacted you right away is a good thing – I suspect that he sees now what he has been missing by not being near you, and this is his way of reaching out and making amends. Is he the perfect dad now? Probably not. And will this make all of the hurt of the past several years go away? Doubtful. But I think it's a step in the right direction and I hope you will accept his gesture and see if things can be better from here on.

I did love your dad very much, and there are so many of his better qualities that I see in you now. Not just your cute smile and those killer dimples (sorry!) but his tender side and passion for life. You got his outgoing nature and optimism for the world that I don't always possess, and while he and I were not meant to be together forever, I am so thankful that we were together long enough for you to join this world. You are truly a blessing to me and to your grand-parents. I hope that as you spend more time with your dad, you will find a way to have the type of relationship I had always wanted for you.

Enjoy your weekend. I will miss you, of course, but am so proud of you and love you more than you will ever know. Love, Mom.

Will stared at the letter and tried to understand what his mom was telling him. Maybe his dad's absence had more to do with him than with Will? He thought back to all the missed ball games, school programs, and church outings where he had secretly hoped he dad would appear unannounced and cheer him from the stands or sidelines. Many times he scanned the crowd, hoping to see him slip in the back door at the very last minute. But that never happened, and the hurt still burned deep. He as not sure that one letter from his mom, and one very short weekend with his dad and new family, was going to make any of that go away. But maybe mom was right —maybe dad was just too young back then, but had seen the error of his ways? Maybe he really should give him a second chance?

Will carefully folded the letter to put it back in the envelope, when he noticed something else still inside. He pulled it out and one of the tears that had been welling in his eyes for the past couple of days finally spilled out onto his cheek. In his hand was a picture he had never seen before, one of those taken at that funny photo booth at the mall. He was just a tiny baby in the picture, only a few weeks old from the look of things, and his dad was holding up in front of the camera with a cheesy grin on his face as he peeked out over Will's shoulder. The resemblance between them really was striking – same nose, same chin, same dimples. But yet will could see how he looked a bit like his mom, too, with her curly hair and pale eyes. He truly was a combo kid, but what he could not get over was the look of love and pride on his dad's face. On the back, written in his dad's handwriting, were the words MY SON! The pride – the joy – all conveyed with that exclamation point. His dad did love him. Really loved him. The shell around Will's heart cracked a bit, just a tiny bit.

After an announcement that it was safe to use electronic devices, Will reached into his backpack for his IPod, more for the isolation than for the music. The Hispanic grandma on the aisle had just come back from a trip to the restroom and was trying in vain to start a conversation. He found a newspaper in the seat pocket and flipped to the entertainment section. Not finding much of value in the hick Des Moines paper, he shoved it back into the pocket. He closed his eyes and let the hypnotic 'thump-thump-thump' of the music lull him into that special place he of- ten retreated to when he we was sad or lonely or confused. The emotions that the letter and photo had stirred were too painful to fully process right now.

Soon the flight attendants were in the aisle, passing out pretzels and drinks. "Would you like some milk Will? Or some juice?"

Will pulled one earbud out of his ear and said in his most sarcastic voice, "I don't like milk, and had juice at home. Thank you anyway." He shoved the earbud back in, closed his eyes, and leaned against the window. Hardly two songs had completed when the flight attendant touched his shoulder and asked him to put his IPod away since they were about to land. Wow, the pilot was not kidding about flying fast! She then informed him that he was to wait until all the other passengers had gotten off the plane and then she would escort him to meet his father. If there had been anyone around him who did not know he was an unaccompanied minor before, they sure did now. Lovely. Why did everyone insist on treating him like a child? He had been forced to grow up a lot these past few years. The fact that he was only about five feet tall did not mean he was a kid on the inside.

Once the plane was on the ground and taxiing toward the gate, Will gathered his belongings and tried to prepare himself mentally for meeting his dad and the new family. What was he supposed to call this new woman – mom? No way! Lily? That sounded too informal and strange. Mrs. Evans? No, that just sounded weird.

Will waited impatiently while the rest of the passengers de- planed, the smell of Memphis barbeque floating down the jet bridge and into the plane. Will's stomach growled at the familiar smell, and he could not wait to get a taste of heaven for himself. One of his favorite childhood memories was when his mom and dad had taken him out for ribs and burnt ends. Even as a small child, he had devoured a rack of ribs by himself, sauce dripping down his chin. The Hispanic grandma reached over and patted his hand, wishing him a fun visit with his dad. If she only knew. Once everyone was off, the flight attendant signaled that it was his turn to leave. She walked up the jet bridge with him, verifying again who was to pick him up. Once at the gate, he saw his dad right away, scanning the passengers and looking anxiously to see him emerge from the tunnel. Will was overcome with a mixture of joy and apprehension. His dad gave him a big hug and marveled at how much he had grown. After showing some ID and signing a couple of forms, they left the gate area and headed toward the baggage claim, where Lily and the girls were waiting. His dad talked non-stop, asking questions about school and summer camp, telling him about the changes at the old house and a surprise the girls had for him. He did not seem to notice that Will was silent or only answering in one or two word phrases. But when they got to the escalator that would take them down to the baggage claim, his dad stopped and looked into his eyes.

"You seem really quiet, Billy. Is everything ok? Or are you tired? Was the flight ok? I know you were delayed a bit, and it's been a long day I imagine."

"Well, dad, first off — no one calls me Billy anymore. I go by Will now. I'm almost a man now, you know."

"Well, of course you are," his dad said with a smile. "The girls will call you Billy because that is what I call you when I talk to them about you. But we can fix that right away."

"You talk to them about me?"

"Of course! You are my number one son, and I will always be proud of you and your accomplishments. It's only natural for me to talk about you all the time. Oh, there they are!"

Will looked down the stairs to see a pretty lady with three cute little girls, all of them waving and the littlest one was jumping up and down. "I see Billy!" she squealed, and Will had a hard time concealing a smile. The middle girl and Lily were both holding bags of his favorite barbeque. "I guess this will be OK" he thought to himself, feeling less nervous than he had anticipated. "But did they have to paint my old room pink?"

BOARDING PASS

Rodriguez, Ana

MEM - DFW

Chapter Seven

Global Air

SEAT NUMBER

19F

Date and Time
JUNE 09, 2017
08:00 PM

Destination: DFW

Chapter Seven

MEM to DFW (Ana Maria)

Ana Eppstein. Ana Maria Eppstein. Ana Maria Rodriguez- Eppstein. Oh, good grief. The pen would run out of ink before she got all of that written out!

She'd been married for almost twenty-four hours, and she was still struck by the novelty of her new surname. Along with the novelty came the uncertainty though. *What is my name now? Who am I now?*

When she ended her broadcast stories for Channel Five in Memphis, the words always came naturally: "This is Ana Maria Rodriguez with Eye-Witness News 5." How long would it take to make the change? Or should she take her producer's advice and continue to go by her maiden name? There was no law that said she had to go by Eppstein. Kyle had said that he didn't mind, but men are so much more sensitive than they appear.

She looked over at her new husband then, smiling faintly at the look of barely contained panic on his face. They couldn't look less alike. Ana was short and curvaceous, brown-skinned, with long, silky black hair and wide dark eyes. Kyle was tall and gangly with long, pale limbs. His hair was sandy brown and his eyes were a shy shade of blue behind rather thick glasses. But beyond their physical differences, their respective body language was like night and day. Ana was folded neatly into her window seat, radiating comfort and excitement to get into the air and on the way toward her honeymoon. Kyle had his long arms crossed over his narrow torso, trying to take up as little space as possible. He was anxious, wound tight enough to snap at any second.

Ana smiled wider, reaching over to cover his tense fingers with her own. It was cruel really that the honeymoon had to come so soon after the wedding. If you think about it, you don't really know a person until you travel with them. Is it really the best idea to test a marriage so soon? As a young-ish and attractive female anchor, Ana always got the top news stories, the ones that required her to travel frequently. Taking a plane was just as comforting and familiar as taking a cab or a bus. If it weren't for the leftover adrenaline from her wedding, and if it weren't for having Kyle next to her radiating anxiety, she would already be asleep, lulled into dreamland by the soothing hum of the jet engine.

This was Kyle's third plane ride ever. The two prior to this had taken place before the attacks on September 11th, so he was naturally a bit high strung, although he did seem to relax minutely at the feel of his new bride's hand on his own.

"Was I whimpering or anything embarrassing out loud?" he asked in a choked whisper.

Ana shook her head and gave him a fond grin. The plane had begun to taxi away from the airport and Kyle's eyes kept focusing beyond her to the window and then back.

"Would you like to see?" she asked kindly, flattening herself back into the cushions. "Or I can close it if you'd rather not."

Kyle's response was a jerky twitch of his chin from left to right. "No, if we're going down, I suppose I'd like to see it coming."

Ana did look at him sternly this time when she noticed the older woman on the other side of Kyle give him a panicked glance. "We're not going down. Everything is going to be great. We will be in Dallas in less than two hours, and Houston a couple hours after that and then we'll be on our way to the dock to get on a gorgeous cruise ship, and before the sun goes down, you and I will have the salty breeze in our faces and a cocktail in each hand."

Kyle smiled at last, showing that one of his incisors was endearingly crooked. "No," he said. "Almost all of that sounds great, except for one thing."

"What?" Ana asked, feeling the plane pick up speed. She wanted to watch the world fall away outside her window, but for the moment Kyle seemed to be relatively calm and she didn't want to disrupt that.

"I can't possibly have a cocktail in both hands, because I'll have at least one of my hands full with one of yours."

Ana giggled and felt a rush of heat in her cheeks. She wasn't normally a giggly girl, but so much had changed in her life so quickly. It hadn't even been a year since the first time she and Kyle had exchanged hesitant but flirty online banter, barely six months since their first phone call. Her friends and family thought she had lost her mind when she agreed to meet him, and many of them wrote her off completely when she announced their engagement just weeks later. But while Ana wasn't usually prone to giggles, she was prone to making decisions and sticking with them. The first time she'd seen Kyle in person, had seen his slight clumsiness and his undeniable charm, well, she hadn't been able to stop herself from falling in love right then and there.

"Oh, Mr. Eppstein, you do say the sweetest things," she murmured.

"Only the truth, my dear Mrs. Eppstein," Kyle replied grandly, giving her a little bow. But then his face tensed as gravity tried to keep them on the ground while the plane rose up into the air. For a moment, Ana lost his attention as he stared out the window. Fortunately, when he did look back at her, he looked more relieved than frightened. "I think I like calling you Mrs. Eppstein," he announced.

Ana gave a half smile. "I was just thinking about that actually. I like it, for my driver's license and all of that. I'll probably keep my maiden name for work though."

As soon as the words were out of her mouth, she wanted them back. Kyle's expression dimmed and his posture slumped as though someone had pulled the plug on him. "Oh," was all he could say.

"I mean, I haven't decided for sure," Ana said, backpedaling quickly. "I'm mostly worried that I'll mess it up, since I'm so used to saying Rodriguez."

"That's understandable," Kyle said, but his tone was a bit flat

"Nothing has to be decided now. Although I'm sure it would be easier for my audience if I kept it the same. And it would save the station from having to rebrand everything."

Kyle's expression was more than a little condescending then. "It's a small local station that I'm sure has enough turnover that rebranding wouldn't be an issue. And change is inevitable. I mean, it's not like we'll be in Memphis forever."

Ana gritted her teeth and focused on her wedding ring. It wasn't large but it was so new and shiny, it dazzled her, even through the thin veil of tears that had just welled up in her eyes. She and Kyle had hit it off so completely that she had never questioned being in love with him or wanting to marry him. But their brief romance hadn't been completely devoid of argument. Perhaps their biggest disagreement involved their future residence. Despite being well traveled, Ana loved Memphis and had no desire to leave. And even though Kyle didn't care for planes, he had seen most of America through a bus window, and found little use in being sentimental over places or things. He could pick up and leave at any time, carrying most of his belongings on his back if need be. Ana hoped that their marriage would show him the appeal of having roots and traditions, but it was hard not to see that he found her profession unimpressive.

Kyle was a writer, and a good one. It was his clever words that had ensnared her in the first place. But Ana wondered now if her career of "reading the news" would ever be good enough for him.

For a long while, Ana stared out the window, watching streaks of clouds rush by. She wasn't having doubts exactly. It only took a few moments of calm thinking to see that Kyle hadn't meant to hurt her feelings. They were different people with different ideas and goals. If they were too much alike, surely one of them would be redundant. So Ana made the conscious effort not to be offended as she scraped around for a change of subject.

It didn't take long at all to forget her moment of annoyance. Kyle's quick humor and almost childlike amusement at the in-flight snack options made Ana laugh out loud. She was really starting to see herself spending the rest of her life with him, but then something happened that had Kyle convinced they wouldn't even make it to Dallas in one piece.

After their empty drink cups had been collected by the flight attendant, Kyle's energy dropped a bit and Ana encouraged him to take a quick nap. They had been rushing around with wedding plans for days now, and it seemed like he was finally ready to crash. While he folded his arms across his stomach and closed his eyes, Ana dug in the seat-back pocket for something to occupy her mind. She found a newspaper that must have been left by a previous passenger, someone from Iowa. One quick glance at the front cover made her wonder what was going on at home. While she wouldn't exactly call herself a workaholic, she did love her job immensely, and the few occasions she'd actually taken vacation time, she had fretted about what news stories she was missing. While Des Moines was clearly not quite as action packed as Memphis, Ana found herself absorbed in the story of the upcoming state fair, when her stomach gave a sharp jolt.

She hadn't noticed at first how the sky outside her window had darkened, but it was obvious now. And the jolt in her stomach hadn't been homesickness or nervousness about her honeymoon. It had been the result of the plane dipping several feet and then stabilizing.

Ana held perfectly still, hoping that the bump hadn't woken Kyle, but the next thing she knew, he was jerking into consciousness beside her with a gasp. She might have been able to convince him he was only imagining things if that had been the only bump, but soon the fuselage shook with mild turbulence as they passed through a storm.

"Oh, Jesus," Kyle whispered, which always made Ana laugh, since he was Jewish. She smothered her smile when she saw the panic in his face and reached for his hand.

"It's totally fine, sweetheart," she assured him. "Just a little turbulence. Nothing to worry about."

He was shaking his head frantically, disagreeing with her but unable to make the words come out of his mouth. Ana could feel the plane changing its trajectory slightly, trying to slice through the clouds at a different, smoother angle. It worked a little, but not for long. With a *ping,* the fasten seatbelt sign came back on, and Kyle's eyes dilated in fear.

"Hey…hey look at me honey," Ana said soothingly. "Focus on my eyes and my voice."

"Oh, we're going down," he muttered tightly.

"Nope, not at all," Ana replied in her gentlest tone. "Planes want to stay in the air. It's just a little bumpy. She put her hands on Kyle's face, trying to hold him steady both literally and figuratively. As he forced himself to breathe and be calm, she let her thoughts wander a bit. She'd watched him shave his face this morning at the hotel, but could already feel the prickles of stubble under her fingertips. It was something she had never noticed or thought about him. "Have you ever grown a beard?"

"What?! You're asking me that now?" Kyle said through clenched teeth.

"I was just curious," she replied, keeping her voice as calm and even as possible. "I can feel a five o'clock shadow already."

"Yeah, I'm a hairy guy," he said distractedly.

Ana frowned as she considered this. They'd been together such a short time, and he'd always been clean shaven and well groomed. She'd given no thought whatsoever to what he would look like with facial hair, or once his hairline began to recede, or if he put on weight in middle age. She'd given no thought to any of it.

Suddenly, Kyle wasn't the only one panicking. "Hey, are you okay?" he asked when Ana had turned abruptly toward the window.

"Fine," she choked out. "It's fine." But inside she was far from fine. She was thinking back to that first day they'd met face to face. He was almost five years her junior, but she hadn't cared because he was steady and serious and mature. He was Jewish, but she hadn't cared because being Catholic didn't really mean much to her besides the occasional Christmas Mass or fancy wedding. He was a bit of a nomad and a loner, but she hadn't cared because he was so content just to be with her and to make a home wherever she was.

Despite all of their differences, they had been a perfect fit for one another, but Ana hadn't thought any of it through. It was as if she expected that glow of togetherness to carry them off into the sunset, but what did that even mean? As the plane jostled and dipped, she knew that reality had always been coming for them, ready to remind them that there would be trials in their marriage as they learned to balance and to compromise with one another. She had fallen in love with Kyle so quickly, had fallen in love with the idea of a wedding and a honeymoon, that she hadn't given nearly enough thought to what it meant to be a wife or a partner. It was surely going to be a lot more than comforting him during turbulence on a plane or agreeing to use his last name at the end of her broadcasts.

"Ana Banana," he said gently, touching her knee and coaxing her to face him again. He still looked nervous, but apparently, the nonchalant attitude of the dozing woman beside him was helping, and he was able to see past his anxiety.

"I'm sorry, babe," Ana whispered. "I just had a little moment there."

"Talk to me."

"It's weird… I just felt your beard coming in and I realized I'd never seen you with a beard. And then I realized I've barely seen you at all. Just a handful of times really. I mean, I fully believe that I know everything I need to know. I love you and I'm always going to love you. But just because

I know what I *need* to know doesn't mean I know everything… Does that make sense?"

"Totally," Kyle replied, his eyes warm and kind now. "There's plenty more I'd like to know. Like last night, when you braided your hair after your shower… What was that all about?"

Ana chuckled and pulled a long strand of her hair over her shoulder. "My hair is bone straight normally. When I braid it while it's wet, it helps make waves like this."

Kyle gave a little hum of understanding. "Well, now I know that. And just so you know, my dad has always had a beard, so I think I avoided it because I associated it with being old."

They both laughed then. "I think you should try it at least once," Ana suggested. "Maybe don't shave on our trip and we'll see if we like it."

"I'm telling you, I'm a hairy guy. It will only take a day or two."

"I can't wait."

"Thank you," Kyle said quietly after a moment.

"For what?" Ana wondered.

"Oh, for so many things. Thank you for loving me and marrying me. But, most currently, thank you for distracting me from the turbulence. I appreciate it."

Ana gave a quick glance out the window and saw that the sky had cleared again and the sailing was smooth. "It was nothing," she said sweetly.

"No, it wasn't nothing at all," Kyle insisted, and he squeezed her hand. She wasn't used to wearing a ring yet, and it pinched a bit, but she kind of liked it. "I know we are very different people," he went on. "I know we come from different backgrounds and have different expectations for what life and happiness really means. I know we're going to fight and disagree. And maybe it sounds crazy, but I'm really looking forward to that."

She grinned. "I don't think that sounds crazy at all."

"So what should we fight about next?" he asked, his smile wide and challenging.

Ana opened her mouth to reply, but just then the captain's voice filled the cabin, advising them that they would be landing in Dallas in just a few moments. "We can fight on the next flight," she promised, tucking the newspaper from Des Moines back into the seat pocket. "For now, let's act like we like each other."

Kyle laughed loudly and gave Ana's hand another squeeze. When she leaned against his shoulder, he rested his head on top of hers, and when the plane hit the runway with a bounce, he barely flinched.

BOARDING PASS

West, Kristin

DFW - MSY

Chapter Eight

Global Air

SEAT NUMBER

19F

Date and Time
JUNE 09, 2017
10:30 PM

Destination: MSY

Chapter Eight

DFW to MSY (Kristen)

She was crying before the plane had started taxiing. Spontaneity wasn't her thing; she always planned things thoroughly. Not that she hadn't planned taking this flight. She just hadn't planned on doing it alone.

For years she'd imagined soaring through the skies from Dallas to New Orleans, but the destination was to be a honeymoon vacation, not a hiding place. She didn't like to run from things. But the last twenty-four hours had changed her, threatened to shake her apart completely, leaving her to put the pieces back in any way they would fit.

The large stocky man in his forties next to her was eyeing her nervously. Like most men of his generation, something genetic was buried within him, triggering a nervous response to a woman crying. And she wasn't some average woman. She was young and beautiful, with wide liquid eyes that just radiated with vulnerability. She was the type of girl that didn't have to try for anything at all; it was just handed to her. And yet she didn't seem to know the power of her own pretty face. Her beauty was the rare and humble type, and the man beside her in seat 19E was practically forced to respond to her.

"The name's Bob Gardner," he said, thrusting a meaty hand toward her. "I always like to introduce myself when I fly alone. That way, if we go down, I wasn't surrounded by strangers."

She turned her eyes to him slowly, blinking back a new set of prickling tears. She wondered if that line was meant to calm her. It was a crummy attempt, and she couldn't help but notice that he wasn't trying to introduce himself to the rather frumpy woman in the aisle seat. But she forced a small smile and reached out to take his hand.

"I'm Kristen," she replied, deliberately leaving off her last name. Bob didn't appear to be the stalker-type that would look her up later, but you never can tell these days. She turned and faced the seatback in front of her, blinking rapidly to keep from disintegrating again.

"So, what's got you headed for the Big Easy?" Bob went on, trying to angle in the seat to face her more directly. Kristen tried not to shrink into the wall. "Business or pleasure?" His face was so genuine that she had to answer.

"Neither," she admitted. "I'm....I'm running away." And the tears built up again.

Bob's face paled slightly and he reached to put his hand on her arm, then pulled it back quickly when he noticed her tense up. "Running away from what, darlin'?"

Kristen leaned her head back against the seat and stared up at the display for the light and air controls. A stream of icy air dried out her tear ducts for a moment. "Joel," she whispered.

Bob's genetic makeup kicked into overdrive again, and his mind seemed to be grinding away in search of a response. "Boyfriend? Did he... hurt you?" Kristen watched his eyes moved over the bits of skin that weren't covered in clothing: wrists, neck, face. The bruise on her heart wouldn't be visible.

"No," she said quickly, not wanting to lie. "Joel's a great guy. The best guy. He's a real hero. He's served in Iraq."

"A soldier? Wow."

"Yes," Kristen agreed with a sigh. Whenever she told someone about Joel's enlistment in the Army, she always got that sort of reaction– awe and pride. It made her feel even more guilty, like she was un-American to hate everything about his devotion to the military. And she didn't really hate it. She was proud of him, of course. But she'd had plans. From the tender age of fifteen, when Joel had first kissed her, she'd known that he was the one. All through high school she'd watched him, searching for a flaw, for a reason to look elsewhere, but they were soulmates through and through.

After graduation, he was supposed to go to UT on a sports scholarship— hopefully baseball. Watching him play football made her queasy. She would work around the clock to save up money. And after he got his Bachelor's degree, they'd get married and honeymoon in New Orleans like they'd always talked about. He'd go on to vet school, and she'd set up house and start having babies, and it would be a small town fairy tale. A dream come true.

But he didn't make the UT baseball team. And his football scholarship didn't pay much. His folks were dead broke after one semester, on the verge of having to sell some of their acreage to keep him enrolled. He did the "right thing." Kristen began to tear up again at the memory.

She could recall it perfectly. It doesn't snow very often in Boonesville, Texas, but it was snowing that day. Huge, puffy flakes of the stuff were floating down onto him where he paused on the porch, sticking in his hair, clinging to his eyelashes. He was breathtaking, but his eyes were strange. They glittered with purpose and with resolution, and for one heart-stopping moment, she thought he was going to propose.

But no. He told her that he'd joined the Army. He was leaving in a week for basic training. And all the plans they'd made were forced to shift.

At first, it really wasn't so bad. She kept working, which was part of the original plan. And she didn't see him much, but she hadn't while he was away at college, either. So they missed each other, but it could have been a lot worse.

But then it actually got worse. In August, they deployed him to somewhere in Iraq. She only vaguely remembered that announcement.

Her whole body had gone numb with fear and with grief, as though she already expected him to come home in a body bag. She hadn't cried then, not until after he was gone. His mother had screamed in agony; his father had clenched his jaw and patted his son bravely on the shoulder. But Kristen had been silent, her mind sluggishly trying to rewrite her future, praying that it could still have a happy ending.

She blinked when Bob put his hand on her arm again. The refreshment cart was parked in the aisle. Kristen didn't even remember the plane taking off.

"Are you thirsty, honey?" the Flight Attendant asked, her eyebrows so high on her forehead they threatened to disappear into her hairline. She'd clearly been standing in the aisle for a while, waiting.

Kristen flushed and ordered a ginger ale to soothe her nervous stomach. She barely tasted it, except to notice that it was cold and wet.

"I didn't mean to pry before, doll," Bob Gardner was saying in his drawling voice. Kristen blinked again. She was having a lot of trouble staying in the present. "It's just that a man hates to see a girl upset. He hates seeing a pretty girl cry, especially over some dumb boy."

"He's not a dumb boy," she retorted, drawing her body slightly in upon itself. "He's a wonderful young man. I'm going to marry him someday."

Bob's eyebrows mimicked the Flight Attendant's from earlier, and Kristen almost smiled at this. He wouldn't understand it, right? How could he?

"Are you married, Bob?" she asked.

"I'm on my third wife, actually. I really like getting married." He guffawed and Kristen really did smile then.

"So you understand what it feels like when love makes everything else seem small and inconsequential. That's how Joel makes me feel... *made* me feel."

"What changed, doll?" he asked her, leaning in like he truly cared.

Her skin crawled a bit at his proximity and the fact that he treated her like a doll, but after all, he was the only one listening. Julie had listened enough and had finally broken her. It was really her fault that all of this had come about.

"Julie," Kristen muttered.

"Julie?" Bob said, confused. "She's not...um, the other woman, is she?"

Kristen couldn't help but laugh at that. It had been far too long since she'd even chuckled; nothing seemed funny to her anymore. But the idea of Joel and Julie, who was thirty-seven and married with six children, being anything other than passing acquaintances made her almost giddy with laughter.

"No, no. She's a coworker of mine," Kristen sputtered. "She's not exactly happy in her marital situation, and she got a little tired of me whining about my perfect boyfriend off defending his country from all enemies, foreign and domestic." There was a sardonic note in her tone as she recited part of Joel's pledge to the Army. Another twinge of guilt flooded over her, and it took Bob's expectant face to remind her that she was in the middle of a story.

"She asked me what I liked most about Joel," she said, and the conversation came rushing back over her like it was yesterday, because it had just been yesterday. Amazing how lifetimes can be lived in just one day.

****

Kristen had gone all dreamy in the face when Julie had asked the question. She thought about what to say. He was beautiful, but that was obvious, not to mention shallow. He was kind and generous, but that wasn't specific to her. He was an amazing kisser, but she felt embarrassed to tell Julie this. No, there was really only one answer to this question.

"When I'm with him, I feel complete. We were made for each other."

But instead of Julie going all soft and giggly with her, she turned stern and cold. "I was afraid you'd say that," the older woman replied.

"What's so wrong with that?" Kristen had argued. "Is it a crime to be a romantic?"

"No," Julie mused. "And it's not a crime to be young and dumb, either, although it ought to be."

That stung. Kristen had considered Julie a good friend, despite the fact that they had almost nothing in common except work at the diner. She didn't try to hide the sadness and anger on her face.

"It happens, once out of a million times, I suppose, that two people love each other equally, and there is a happily ever after down the road," Julie preached as she filled salt and pepper shakers with a practiced hand. "And for all I know, you and Joel are that one couple. But more often than not, there is an imbalance. When you realize that it's worth working through that imbalance, you have a relationship that survives. When you can't, well, you become one of the majority that get divorced. Heck, tons of couples aren't even getting married anymore. They're just shacking up to save the drama when it ends. Not that you could get away with that in this small town and still expect to show your faces in church on Sunday." She laughed, and Kristen felt herself blush and then glow with irritation. What did this woman know about her and Joel? How could she just assume that they were not perfect for each other? What had happened to her that she was so cynical and jaded?

"Look, I love him, okay? And we are that one in a million. We're perfect together and we're going to get married and have babies, and everything's going to be great."

Julie stopped her work for a second and leveled a hard glance at her young coworker. "Can I ask you something personal?"

"You're going to anyway," Kristen retorted, stacking packets of jelly into the metal holder. She always made a point to separate the jellies from the jams, not that any of her customers would know the difference or care.

"What is something that you want to do with your life, something that doesn't involve Joel?"

Kristen made a face, but the honesty in Julie's expression made her actually consider the question. Every avenue of her plans had Joel at the heart of them, and that was the point, right? It apparently took her too long to answer, because Julie was looking smug.

"My point exactly. You've wrapped your whole future around that kid, and I'm certainly not going to say he's not worth it, because he's a doll. I love him, you know I do. But here's the deal, honey. Marriage is tough, and even if it works out, it not always perfect. It's rarely perfect, actually. You get a few top notch vacations or anniversaries, a few great memories, and then it's all about the kids and what they're doing and where they're going to school. And then it will be about their kids. You never get to be just you. This is your chance to be you, and I worry that you're wasting it."

"I know this may sound backward to you, but I don't want anything for myself except to be Joel's wife and to have his kids and keep his house. I've known that since I was fifteen. That's who I am."

"I'm not trying to be mean, Kris, you know that." Julie insisted. "I just want you to really think. Is there nothing that you wanted to do, something that was just for you? Did you ever want to take a class, or learn an instrument, or take a trip by yourself, just because you wanted to go? Maybe I'm just cynical because my mom was a single parent, and she taught me not to rely on a man, to be able to stand on my own two feet. It's why I work here, even though I don't have to and Lord knows I don't have time for it, what with the kids and all their sports. But I hate when young girls go on and on about how a man completes them."

"But he does complete me," Kristen argued. "We match up perfectly. We were meant to be together."

"I don't doubt that you're supposed to be together, honey. I've seen the way you look at each other. I know if anyone's got a chance to be that one in a million, it's you two. But you have to be complete on your own! You have to know who you are, to be able to do what you want to do, just because it makes you happy. Now, I'll ask you again, is there nothing you ever wanted for yourself?"

Kristen said the first thing that popped into her head, the only thing she'd ever really wanted. She wanted to go to New Orleans. Born and raised a small town girl, she'd never had the urge to go anywhere. Content to read about other places in books, no other city or state or country had ever called to her. Except for New Orleans. She couldn't explain it to anyone, because she didn't really understand it herself, but she'd seen a documentary on television when she was about thirteen, all about Mardi Gras. She didn't truly understand the whole drunken revelry or the beads in exchange for nudity, but the colors were so overwhelming.

Boonesville is vast and brown for the better part of the year, and vast and greenish-brown during the late spring and early summer. The French Quarter on the documentary had shone like a Christmas tree in April, bursting with color like ripe fruit. Something tangible had awoken inside of her upon seeing that, and ever since, she'd been obsessed with the city. She'd even convinced Joel that they would honeymoon there. She'd found the best hotels and restaurants for them to hit while they were there. He'd imprinted on her dream, bit it had been hers alone once.

As Kristen gushed to Julie about her desires, she began to finally see what Julie had told her. Life before Joel was a hazy inconsequential memory to her. Except for this one thing. This trip, this place was the one thing she had that was her own.

The seed was planted. She had excitedly packed her bright pink camouflage suitcase, and she was ready to go to Atlanta to meet Joel. He was due back stateside anytime now. After months of lonely separation, he was coming back to her. And all of the sudden, she felt trapped by his return.

****

She looked with her big, panicked eyes at Bob, who had listened to her story with rapt attention. "So you see, after all those months of wishing for the clock to move faster, suddenly I was out of time. I know that I could still go to New Orleans with him after we were married, but who knows when that will be? We've had to keep pushing the date because of his tours being extended. And who wants to be married to a man who's never home, who's off getting shot at every five minutes?"

Bob looked on mutely, trying to emote with only his face because he didn't seem to be able to trust his words. Kristen realized that her questions were mostly rhetorical anyway, and plunged ahead.

"So, I had this crazy idea to just go to New Orleans. Now. By myself. Have that thing that's mine. And maybe I come back and maybe I don't. I was almost decided; I almost had decided to come. And then he called me."

Bob watched as her face glowed and her whole frame seemed to relax. "His voice...oh his voice on the phone, and not some crappy international connection that's bouncing off nine different spy satellites. I could hear him breathing, smiling. He was mine and he was home. I forgot all about New Orleans. I went to the airport so that I could go to Atlanta and get him. Bring him home with me for however long he can stay."

"But something happened," Bob guessed, seeing as how she was most definitely not on a plane to Atlanta right now.

Kristen's face contorted and the tears pooled again. Bob tensed and apologized with this eyes for setting her off again. "It was a Marine and his wife at the security station. He had two daughters with him. They were all crying and hugging, but the little girls were so brave about it. You could tell they'd done this before. Daddy was headed off to the front lines. Again. Even after he'd settled down and gotten married, he'd stayed in the service. He kept putting himself in harm's way. And I get that it's noble," she said quickly before Bob could retort, though he probably wouldn't have. "I get that it's unbelievably brave, and that someone has to go, but I don't want it to be Joel. And worse than that, I don't want to be that woman left behind here, with children, wondering every day if she's going to get a phone call from him or if it will be from some faceless person telling her that her husband is dead. Even if he keeps coming home safe, I didn't sign on to be a soldier's wife. No one asked me if I wanted that. He just did it. To help us get the future we wanted, yes. But I would have changed my dreams, maybe. If it would have kept him safe *with me,* I would have changed my dreams."

She put a shaking hand to her face and pushed away a couple of tears that managed to fall past her eyelashes. She sniffed once.

"But I watched that woman walk away from the gate, looking like she had been beaten, she was so torn up. And her little girls, for all of their bravery, they were crying. And I just knew I had to get out. Out of this stupid boring state. Out of this fake future that's never going to happen because Joel will never be home to enjoy it. I marched up to the gate and changed my ticket. And now I'm here. With you. Crying all over you, I'm so sorry."

"That's alright, doll," he said quietly, not quite truthfully perhaps. "You'll like New Orleans. It's just as colorful and loud and exciting as you think. You missed Mardi Gras, of course, but there's always a party going on somewhere."

"Thank you, Bob," she said with a sniff. "Thank you for listening."

She turned away from him and began to rifle through the seat pocket in front of her. Amazed, she felt the tiniest hint of a smile working its way up within her. Even though her cheeks were still damp with tears, she felt lighter, as though just speaking her fears and her frustrations had lifted weights from her shoulders. She still didn't know the answers. She still wasn't remotely sure that taking this random trip was the right thing to do, but for this next half hour or so, she didn't feel the need to dwell on it. There wasn't a whole lot she could do about it at 30,000 feet, anyway.

The Sky Mall catalog amused her for a few minutes, but the gadgets all began to blur together for her, none of them holding her attention. Kristen managed to waste another few minutes pawing through a tattered newspaper that turned out to be from Des Moines, Iowa. She didn't really read the thing; she only pondered how something that had been printed on a press overnight in Iowa had travelled so far in just one day. Feeling poetic, she imagined the parallel between the newspaper's journey and her own over the past day – some sort of random, crisscrossing trek from one extreme to another. Instead of putting the paper back, she tucked it into her purse, not entirely sure why she was doing it.

The only thing left to occupy the last few minutes of the flight was to strike up more conversation with Bob. Or else work the crossword puzzle in the in-flight magazine. She stole a glance at her neighbor and found him buried in a John Grisham novel, so she opted for the crossword instead. To her dismay, most of it had been worked by previous passengers, many of them judging by the varied handwriting and pen colors. It was just as well – she was almost sure she did not have a pen of her own handy.

On the verge of closing the magazine and attempting to grab a nap, something caught her eye. She couldn't quite explain how she noticed it, but one small character stood out. The letter Z, crossed through the middle like some people do. Like Joel does. The ache she'd felt earlier welled up like a slap in the face, and she had to lean back and slam her eyes shut just to keep from whimpering at the pain.

But the hits just kept coming. Breathing in deeply, she realized that she could smell him. Someone wearing Joel's cologne was close by, or had been here recently. The sharp scent triggered so many memories. Kristen opened herself up to the dizziness and kept breathing it in, kept feeling him. And she was right back to the way she felt when she'd heard his voice yesterday. That same fuzzy sensation that made her smile at just the thought of him.

Panic followed swiftly after. She was going the wrong direction. Joel would be waiting for her in Atlanta, and she was only moments from New Orleans. Just thinking about the sparkling city added another layer to her confusion. She could feel the streets of the Lower Nine beckoning her with their ghost stories. Could Joel's hold on her be stronger than that of her one childhood dream?

"Bob!" she said suddenly, and the big man jerked in surprise. He used a thick finger as a bookmark and turned to her expectantly. "Sorry to scare you. I'm just trying to work out a little internal drama. Will you answer a question for me?"

"Of course, doll," Bob replied, his voice having transformed from intrusive to comforting over the length of the flight.

"Do you think I did the right thing? Do you think me going to New Orleans is the right thing to do?

He winced briefly, wanting to answer anything but that, but then he laughed good-naturedly. "Well, my dear, you have to understand that I'm a serial monogamist. When I fall in love, I fall hard and I commit. Until she leaves me for one reason or another." He chuckled, showing just a touch of sadness in his eyes. "So, I'm always in favor of love winning out. It's a gamble, sure. But it's so worth it. So I think you play around in the city for a few days and remember that time before all of your decisions took your soldier into account. Have time with you and the city lights. And then you go on home to that boy and tell him to make an honest woman out of you. Tell him what you told me, that you'd move heaven and earth to be with him, but that he's got to be there. If that's what you want, if he's what you want, then you need to tell him. That way, even if he does deploy again, he'll know for sure that you're the one. He'll put aside anything that keeps you two apart. I know that's what I'd do, if a pretty girl said those things to me." He smiled sheepishly at her and she turned away, letting the tears fall helplessly.

"Thank you, Bob," she whispered.

"Don't mention it," he replied gruffly. Just then, the plane began its descent.

Kristen let the next several minutes spinning out in a sort of recap of the last day. She heard Julie's words, and Bob's. She recalled the Marine parting ways with his family. She basked in the memory of Joel's voice on the phone. Everything felt obvious, like the right decision was directly in front of her. At the same time, no plan seemed to be better than the other.

Bob patted her lightly on the shoulder when they'd emerged into the terminal. He trotted off toward the baggage claim area, leaving Kristen standing in a sea of commuters. They parted around her as though she was a rock in a swift stream, no one really bothering to wonder why she looked so sad, so confused.

She was in New Orleans, but it just looked like another airport, nearly identical to the one she'd left just hours before. Joel was in Georgia, probably too anxious to fall asleep, assuming they'd be together soon. The desire to go and find him made her take a step forward. But the call of her old dreams wouldn't let her go any further than that. She couldn't say how long she just stood there.

"Can I help you find something, dear?" a guy in a uniform asked her, startling Kristen from her thoughts. She turned to look at him, taking in none of his appearance except that he wore a polyester vest and a nametag that reflected the fluorescent lighting in an authoritative way. "The baggage claim is up that way," he gestured, his thick Cajun accent twisting the words charmingly. "Or I can point you to your connecting gate."

"No, no, I've got it. I know where I want to go. Thank you."

And she began walking, smiling, as she became more confident of her decision with every step.

Epilogue

Jean Robert' LaFontaine (JR)

Jean Robert' leaned back in his chair in the baggage handlers' lounge, his long legs propped on the lunch table. There was just one more flight to unload tonight before his shift ended, and then he could head home to his wife and five kids. He was scheduled to have the next four days off, and was anxious for some rest and relaxation. Most everyone was already gone from the 3-11 shift, but he and his buddy Manny had volunteered to stay and offload the late flight from Dallas. When the radio squawked to let them know the plane was within range, JR grabbed his knee pads and headgear and stepped out onto the tarmac.

Manny climbed up into the belly of the plane to put the bags onto a conveyor belt that led down to JR's truck. JR waited on the ground to stack the luggage onto a cart and then drive them back into the terminal. The bags were unloaded from the plane quickly and he was ready to head back inside when he noticed a small pink bag that had fallen from the conveyor belt onto the tarmac. He hopped from the truck and tossed the bag into the back. Hot pink camouflage? Well, at least it was not the standard black bag that so many travelers insisted on using these days.

The bags were quickly put onto another conveyor belt that would take them upstairs to the waiting passengers. After clocking out and saying goodnight to Manny, JR chatted with the staff coming on shift and reviewed his schedule for the following week. Still bragging about having the next four days off, he walked across the parking lot towards his car. Noticing something white on the ground, he stopped to pick up a newspaper that someone had dropped, and tossed it into the nearest trashcan. His eye caught the masthead – *Des Moines Register.* "That's pretty unusual, finding a paper so far from home. Bet it's had quite a day," and he walked off into the intoxicating New Orleans night.

Printed in the United States
By Bookmasters